'Engel's pacing is breathless she covers three generations in under 200 pages but just as frequently gives way to heart- and time-stopping moments. *Infinite Country* is poised to be one of the most stirring page-turners of the year' **A.V. Club**

'Clear, moving, and perfectly calibrated, *Infinite Country* follows the members of one mixed-immigration status family as they navigate dreams, distance, and the bonds of love and memory. Patricia Engel is a stunning writer with astonishing talents' **Lisa Ko, author of *The Leavers***

'Engel's gaze is intensely intimate but never voyeuristic, and her prose, while sparse and digestible, is full of poignant observations . . . Perfect for readers of Isabel Allende and Valeria Luiselli, this book offers readers from all walks of life a searingly timely perspective on the challenges faced by those in pursuit of a dream' *Book Reporter*

'An intriguing, compact tale, rife with both real-life implications and spiritual significance . . . Engel does a marvelous job of rendering these characters as individuals, each with a unique story' *BookPage*

'Exquisitely written and composed . . . Heartbreaking and profound, this is a must read' *Boston Magazine*

'Powerful and poignant, Infinite Country crystallizes the questions we are asking today about migration, family, and our vision of the future. Patricia Engel has written a memorable and brutally honest response to the simplistic notion of what constitutes the American Dream' **Maaza Mengiste, author of *The Shadow King***

'*Infinite Country* is both a timely and timeless novel. In beautiful prose, Patricia Engel brings to life the courage and complexity of the immigrant experience, illuminating the hardship of life between two countries and two languages, and the search for family and belonging' **Jennifer Clement, author of *Gun Love***

Praise for *Infinite Country*:

'A knockout of a novel . . . we predict [*Infinite Country*] will be viewed as one of 2021's best' *O, The Oprah Magazine*

'A poignant and beautifully written tale' *Financial Times*

A *Grazia* 'Best Book of 2021'

'An exquisitely told story of family, war, and migration, this is a novel our increasingly divided country wants and needs to read' **R.O. Kwon,** *Electric Literature*

'An exceptionally powerful and illuminating story about a Colombian family torn apart by war and migration' **Reese Witherspoon**

'[a] powerful and intimate account of life in the diaspora' **Refinery29, 'Best New Books of 2021'**

'Lyrical . . . Weaving together the different experiences of each family member, *Infinite Country* offers a poignant account that blends both tragedy and victory' *The Glossary* (UK)

'A heartbreaking portrait of a family dealing with the realities of migration and separation' *Time*, **'Best Books of March 2021'**

'At once a sweeping love story and tragic drama, *Infinite Country* . . . promises to deliver what *American Dirt* could not: an authentic vision of what the American Dream looks like in a nationalistic country' *Elle*

'A gorgeous, moving novel' *New York Post*

'Engel movingly captures the shadow lives of undocumented migrants . . . a profound, beautiful novel' *People Magazine*

'[Engel is] a gifted storyteller whose writing shines even in the darkest corners' *The Washington Post*

'The prose is serpentine and exciting ... [with] intimate and meticulously rendered descriptions of Andean landscapes and mythology, of Colombia's long history of violence ... a compulsively readable novel' *New York Times Book Review*

'A diamond-sharp novel ... With stunning sentences, vivid language, and a pace that will leave you breathless, *Infinite Country* is steeped in myth and rich in both depth and beauty. There's a not a single word misplaced in this book' *The Today Show*

'Engel's sweeping novel gives voice to three generations of a Colombian family torn apart by man-made borders ... Gorgeously woven through with Andean myths and the bitter realities of undocumented life, *Infinite Country* tells a breathtaking story of the unimaginable prices paid for a better life' *Esquire*

'A memorable line 'It was her idea to tie up the nun' launches the narrative with the force of a cannon as it switches back and forth between the present and the past ... Told by a chorus of voices and perspectives, this is as much an all-American story as it is a global one' *starred* *Booklist*

'An outstanding novel of migration and the Colombian diaspora ... Engel's sharp, unflinching narrative teems with insight and dazzles with a confident, slyly sophisticated structure. This is an impressive achievement' *starred* *Publishers Weekly*

'Engel's vital story of a divided Colombian family is a book we need to read ... The rare immigrant chronicle that is as long on hope as it is on heartbreak' *starred* *Kirkus Reviews*

First published in the United States by Avid Reader Press,
an imprint of Simon & Schuster, Inc., 2021
First published in Great Britain by Scribner,
an imprint of Simon & Schuster UK Ltd, 2021
This paperback edition published in 2022

1 3 5 7 9 10 8 6 4 2

Simon & Schuster UK Ltd
1st Floor
222 Gray's Inn Road
London WC1X 8HB

Simon & Schuster Australia, Sydney
Simon & Schuster India, New Delhi

www.simonandschuster.co.uk
www.simonandschuster.com.au
www.simonandschuster.co.in

A CIP catalogue record for this book is available from the British Library

PB ISBN: 978-1-3985-0665-7
EBOOK ISBN: 978-1-3985-0663-3
AUDIO ISBN: 978-1-3985-0664-0

Interior design by Ruth Lee-Mui
Printed in the UK by CPI Group (UK) Ltd, Croydon, CR0 4YY

MIX
Paper from
responsible sources
FSC
www.fsc.org
FSC® C171272

INFINITE COUNTRY

PATRICIA ENGEL

SCRIBNER

LONDON NEW YORK SYDNEY TORONTO NEW DELHI

For my parents and my brother

Mi patria es la tierra.

—Arturo Salcedo Martínez, *Sentido de Patria*

Diasporism is my mode.

—R. B. Kitaj, *First Diasporist Manifesto*

ONE

It was her idea to tie up the nun.

The dormitory lights were cut every night at ten. Locked into their rooms, girls commanded to a cemetery silence before sleep, waking at dawn for morning prayers. The nuns believed silence a weapon, teaching the girls that only with it could they discover the depths of their interior without being servants to the temptations of this world.

To be fair, the nuns were not all terrible. Some, Talia liked very much. She even admired how they managed to turn the condemned penitentiary population into mostly orderly damitas. It was a state facility. A prison school for youth offenders. Not a convent and no longer a parochial school. The lay staff reminded the sisters to aim for secularity, but on those missioned mountains, the nuns ran things as they pleased.

During the day, under the nuns' watch, the girls practiced their downcast gazes. They attended classes, therapy sessions, meditation groups, completed chores uniformed in gray sweats, hair pulled back. Forbidden from gossip and touching, but they did both when out of sight.

At night, in the blackness of their dormitory, they gathered to whisper in shards of windowpane moonlight. When the nuns patrolled the hall outside their room, they became masterful mutes, reading lips, inventing their own sign language, moving quiet as cats, creeping like thieves. They listened for the nuns' footsteps on the level below, sensing vibrations on the wooden floor planks; the search for rule breakers, disruptors their guardians would schedule for punishment at daybreak.

The night of the escape, the girls made purposeful noise so the nun on duty would come tell them to be quiet. Sister Susana was on the nightshift. There were many latecomer nuns at the facility leftover from some other failed life. The rumor was Sister Susana was married until her husband divorced her because she couldn't have children.

The plan originated with Talia. Or maybe her father deserved the credit. That afternoon she was given rare permission to phone him from the administrative office. Family contact was restricted, since the staff believed they could be a girl's worst influence. Talia hoped to hear Mauro say he found a way to free her, have her sentence lifted. Paid a fine or convinced one of the rich residents of the apartment building where he worked as a janitor to call in a favor on her behalf.

One never knows who might be listening, especially in a quasi jail for minors, some of whom were murderers on the verge. Talia and Mauro were careful with their words. He'd tried everything, he said. There was nothing more he could do. She understood. Liberating herself from the prison, and the country, would be up to her.

With the help of another girl, she spent an hour ripping bedsheets, twisting them tight as wire, thin as rope. She counted to one thousand in the darkness, then gave the signal for the other girls to start shouting, "Fire! Fire! Fire!"

Sister Susana appeared in the doorway. Talia waited to catch her from behind with a pillowcase over the head. They'd cut breathing holes because they weren't trying to kill anyone, only to paralyze with fright. Talia held the nun while the others tied her to a chair with the shredded sheets, her breath hot on Talia's hands as another girl shoved a sock between her teeth to gag screams.

When Talia arrived to the prison school a month earlier, Sister Susana had called her into her office and told the fifteen-year-old she'd studied her life, as if that file of police jottings and psychological assessments on her desk could reveal anything that mattered.

"You're not like other girls here," she began.

Yes, I am, Talia wanted to say. She didn't want to be singled out, treated as an exception if it meant putting the other girls down.

"I believe it was your desire for justice that led you to do an awful thing. But you badly injured a man. You could have blinded him."

A pause. The rattle of voices in the cafeteria down the hall. She knew Sister Susana was waiting for a response. A denial perhaps. More likely an admission of guilt. The nuns were always scavenging for remorse.

"Do you want to change? With faith and discipline anything is possible."

Talia was not stupid, so she said yes.

The girls locked Sister Susana in their room with the same key she used against them each night. Nobody would look for her or for the girls until morning. The sisters and lay staff were in charge of their correction and safety. There were security guards on the property, but they were all men, so the nuns made them stay by the front gates to prevent the girls from developing crushes and the guys from trying to seduce them, as if that were a greater menace than an uprising, the girls taking the building under siege as happened all the time in men's prisons; the illusion that women are safer among women.

The girls returned to their silence. Twelve to a room, the building held four dormitories in different corners of the building, each under the patrol of rotating nuns and staff. They knew the other girls. They had classes and meals with them every day. That night they wouldn't worry about them, though, and Talia no longer worried about the girls with whom she planned her escape. The careless or slow would jeopardize her freedom. They would flee to boyfriends, friends, or relatives willing to hide them. But she had less than one week to get back to Bogotá, to the airport and out of Colombia.

When they hurried down the service stairs, out through the back garden to run across the sports field and over the concrete wall spiked with broken glass to the road as plotted, she broke away from the cluster, hustling east past the courtyard, through the gate into the forested hills spiraling down toward the valley.

Halting in a shadow before her final bolt, she saw the guards in the watchhouse by the prison driveway, hypnotized by the glare of a small TV. She'd assumed them to be some kind of police. They carried guns, and the girls believed they could chase and shoot them in the legs if they were caught trying to escape.

She ran alone in the fog, through dirt and thicket. It hadn't rained in a few days, so there was little mud. She heard night creatures. Frogs. Owls. Hissing insects. Through the tree canopy, the rustle of rodents or bats. An hour passed. Maybe two. Lights congealed. An illuminated road laced the forest curtain. She followed until she heard barking dogs warn she'd come too close to the fences of a finca, so she moved down the hill to the street.

If you'd passed her in a car as she walked, small in her baggy captivity uniform, an expression more lost than determined, you might not have thought her a fugitive from the school for bad girls up the mountain, the place said to reform criminals in the making.

She came to a gas station far from any route the other girls would have taken, approached a grandfatherly man in worn jeans filling up his truck tank, and asked for a ride.

"Where are you headed?"

"Anywhere but here." She only knew the facility was somewhere in Santander and the nearest town was San Vicente de Chucurí.

The man scratched his beard. "A word of advice. Don't ever tell a stranger you'll go *anywhere*."

"I need to head south. I hope to make it all the way to Tunja, but I'll take any route to get there." She didn't want the man to know she was headed to the capital in case police asked him questions later. At least from Tunja she knew she could find her way home.

The man said he was going to Aratoca but would drop her off in Barichara. Lots of tourists and buses passed through, so she could likely find a way south from there. He wasn't leaving until sunrise though. He needed to sleep a few hours before getting back on the road.

She didn't want to return to the woods. Before long, the police would have turned over every vine on the mountain searching for girls. She told the man she'd wait with him if that was okay. When he finished fueling, he pulled the truck into an unpaved lot behind the station and invited her to follow. She waited as he reached to open the passenger door, then dropped his own seat back, leaning into sleep.

"You can do the same," he said, eyes closed. "I won't touch you. I give you my word. I have two daughters. Not as young as you, but they're still my babies."

Her hesitation was mostly for show. Even if he hadn't made such a pledge she would have done the same, climbing into the truck, nudging her seat as flat as she could so her head fell below the window line. Disappeared.

•   •   •

It happened behind a cafetería near the El Campín fútbol stadium. Talia went to meet her friend Claudia at the end of her shift so they could see a movie together. She waited in the alley beside the restaurant, smoking a cigarette with a waiter she thought was kind of cute though he sometimes spit when he spoke and used slang she didn't understand. Two of the kitchen guys were also on break, talking in a corner of the alley near the dumpster.

Talia was bragging that she'd soon be leaving Bogotá for good. Her mother had finally paid for her plane ticket north. She'd meet the other half of her family. See New York and all that cool gringo shit from movies and music videos. How lucky she was, the waiter said, and asked her to write him all about it. She agreed, knowing she never would.

The kitchen guys were crouched on the ground looking at something by the garbage cans. The pavement was covered in disgusting muck and roach cadavers. One of the guys stepped away to go back into the kitchen. Talia saw a small cat where he'd been standing, orange and matted. She and the waiter walked over to get a better look. She was inclined to take it home, convince her father it would make good company for him after she left the country.

It happened in seconds. The kitchen guy who went inside returned with a bowl, walking quickly, and before anyone could ask what the hell, he poured a smoky liquid over the cat. It convulsed under the steam. Flesh cooked. Fur shriveling. Dead without a sound.

"What did you do?" Talia yelled, but the man only laughed, kicking the dead animal like a crumpled can toward the trash bins.

She can only describe what came over her as a subterranean reflex. A pressure to act that coursed through her as if from the earth.

She took off through the kitchen door. The waiter and the kitchen guys must have thought she went to complain to Claudia. Instead, she went to the stoves, found a pot of hot cooking oil, took a large bowl off the counter just as the man had done, dipped it into the pot, and felt the steam graze her wrist. She walked out to the alley, and when she was close enough, turned the bowl, aiming the splash at the cat killer, oil dripping from scalp to shoulders, arms to hands. He dropped to the ground howling, blistering, palms and fingers soon swollen as yams.

They didn't have to restrain her because she didn't try to run. She knew he wouldn't die. If she'd meant to kill him she would have heaved the whole pot off the stove or reached for a knife and not just a bowl. The kitchen workers crowded around him and started praying while Talia leaned against the building and waited for whatever would come next.

The ambulance arrived quickly. The police took longer, which was normal. Paramedics wrapped the man—by this time she'd learned his name was Horacio—in a shroud while he fell into shocked delirium. The police handcuffed her and took statements from witnesses. Claudia came out and begged to know what happened while other employees, customers, and street people also tried to get a look.

They held Talia in police custody over the day and night that her crime made the city news. Just a quick mention on the evening TV reports and a few paragraphs in the local section of the print editions. They held her in a dim room with four other girls who said they were arrested on drug charges, though who knew for sure. The girls kept asking what Talia had done to be arrested, and she replied that she didn't know, until one of the girls pushed Talia's head into the toilet in the corner, so she told them the truth.

By morning she was released to her father's supervision, an advantage of being a first-time offender. The press had already moved from the story of the teenage girl burning a man onto actual murders and the political corruption scandal of the week. But she saw the newspaper clippings her father had saved at home, including color photos of charred Horacio, his face fried to a pink, satiny crepe peeking from beneath the bandages. Without revealing her name, journalists wrote about the girl who attacked him in a baseless rage, adding that she would be tried and sentenced as a minor even if her crime demonstrated adult malice. There was no mention of the cat.

Talia considered how people who do horrible things can be victims, and how victims can be people who do horrible things. The witnesses who spoke to reporters said it was as if a lever had been turned in the girl they'd seen around the restaurant many times before waiting for her friend. Even Claudia was quoted saying she couldn't believe her dear friend was capable of such cruelty. Talia wondered if she meant it. Claudia's mother was also in the United States, and, like Talia, she was left in Colombia to be raised by her grandmother. They were good students. Their only crimes were occasionally taunting weaker girls in school, that time they shoplifted sunglasses from El Centro Andino, or lying to boys they met from other barrios, making up names and accents that didn't belong to them.

She'd gone through a series of evaluations when admitted to the facility on the mountain. She was never given any medications. Not even when a doctor asked if she'd ever pondered suicide and she answered, "Who hasn't?" The therapists and caseworkers were perplexed. How could a girl with no history of delinquency or aggression commit such a violent act? Most of the girls in the prison school had pages of predictive conduct behind them, from drug use, robbery, setting fires, to running with gangs or abusing their siblings or parents. The impulse to hurt Horacio must have come from somewhere, they agreed, but Talia was exemplary at home and school.

Her record undeniably clean. They ran down a list of traumas. Rape. Abuse. Neglect. Displacement from the armed conflict. Orphaning. None applied to Talia. She told them her mother was abroad and sent her back to Colombia when she was a baby. But this particular family condition was so common it couldn't possibly be considered trauma.

Talia rolled the passenger window down to release the dank truck air, then rolled it back up to keep out the bugs. Every hour through the bleed of green hills, the old man pulled over to rag-wipe grime from the windshield. They spoke for stretches, then fell quiet. In the talking part, he told her he used to drive cargo for a yanqui fruit company till accused of skimming shipments. He swore to her he never pocketed a single banana.

"We're all innocent," she said. Sometimes she believed this.

After some time, without lifting his eyes from the road, he told her, "Whatever you're running from must be serious. You've got no money and no phone and haven't asked to borrow mine to let anyone know you're okay." When this failed to prompt a confession, he tried again. "You can trust me. I'm a wonder at keeping secrets."

"My grandmother who raised me is dying of a disease that stole her memory, so now she's lost in time and everyone is a stranger." All of this was fact except that her grandmother was already dead and Talia would have given her lungs for Perla to take another breath in this world. "My parents won't let me visit her out of revenge because she never approved of their marriage. They took my phone and my money. I had to run away just to see her before she leaves this life. She may not recognize me when I arrive, but she will know in some part of her that someone who loves her is with her."

He brushed a tear from an eye, admitting his greatest regret was having left his wife, the mother of his daughters, for another woman. When he realized his error it was too late. She wouldn't take him back. He was on his way to Aratoca to see her, still hoping for forgiveness.

"What does your other woman have to say about that?"

"Nothing. She died."

They drove past signs for towns she'd only ever seen on maps and knew she would never see again. The truck came to a check-point, slowing to a stop.

"Military now," the old man remarked, "but not so long ago it was guerrilla, like there's a difference. The worst part is these kids have no manners."

A young camouflaged soldier approached his window. "Where are you headed?"

"Aratoca. We live there."

He tipped his machine gun toward Talia. "Who's the girl?"

"My niece."

The soldier stared at her. "Is that true?"

"He's my father's brother." Her mind flashed with the portrait of another life, one with aunts and uncles and cousins, a life she never knew.

The soldier stepped back, letting the mouth of his weapon slide toward the earth, signaling ahead to the other officers barricading the road to let the truck through. The downhill road smelled of gasoline, smoke, wet soil. She remembered when the police came for her at home. She'd asked if she could pack some clothes, but they'd said there was no need. She'd thought of running then, but there was only one way out of the apartment building and the officers were blocking it. Then the long drive up the mountain. One of six recently sentenced girls carted like livestock, wrists bound by plastic cuffs. The van windows blackened with paint but the scent of the unencumbered earth told her she was far from home.

TWO

The social worker described the compound like a summer camp, a small boarding school in the hills of Santander. A retreat, even if operated by the government. There were academic classes so the girls wouldn't fall behind when, time served, they were free to return to their normal schools. She told Mauro he should be grateful his daughter wasn't treated the same as girls from lower estratos, comunas, or invasiones, the ones usually sent to rougher facilities. Talia, she said, could pass for middle class, and this is why she was sentenced to only six months, given a path to redemption, even as Mauro argued this was a country of not second but hundredth chances for the chosen; a nation of amnesiacs where narcotraficantes become senators and senators become narcotraficantes, killers become presidents and presidents become killers.

Mauro knew what it was to be locked away. He'd never spoken of it with any of his children, with Elena or Perla. Men corralled in a warehouse cold as a meat locker. The rationing of showers and blankets and food. The dream of release, not to Elena or the children, but to the land the gringos threatened to banish him to as if it were a return to hell.

Home.

When she was small Talia often asked her father the meaning

of the word. *Home.* Sometimes she understood it meant a house or an apartment, the place a person returned to at the end of a long day. The place where one's family lived even if they left it a long time ago. The place one felt most comfortable. All of these notions contradicted her first sense of it. Home, to Talia, was a space occupied by her grandmother Perla. A place Mauro came to visit when she and her mother, Elena, over the international wires, permitted it.

Elena was far away with Talia's siblings, Nando and Karina. When Talia heard her mother's voice over the phone she often spoke of Colombia as home but quickly added, so her daughter wouldn't misunderstand, that the United States was home now too. "It's also *your* home," she'd tell Talia, "because you were born here."

Years later, when it was just Talia and Mauro living together in Perla's old house, she pressed her body close against her father's chest when he came to her room to give her la bendición before sleep. "You are my home," she'd said. "Even if my mother makes me leave you, I will always come back to you."

She was a girl who perceived leaving for North America as a distant threat. Something she could not imagine she would ever want. One day it was different. Mauro noticed Talia's face when they watched gringo movies or television programs with subtitles. That unmistakable, irrevocable fascination. The way she started inserting English words into their conversations. He saw the longing take hold, crisp disdain for her familiar yet stale life with him.

He blamed himself for the way he made both Elena and Talia resent their country. His tendency of pointing out evidence of hypocrisy as if their colonized land was more doomed than any other. He wanted to take it all back. The malignant seeds he planted in Elena, who, until she met Mauro, never saw another future beyond helping Perla run the lavandería, who'd only ever traveled as far as

Villavicencio on a school trip, for whom a trip to Cartagena was as inconceivable as one to Rome.

Mauro was the one who put it in her head that Bogotá was just another pueblo masquerading as a metropolis and there was more to discover. In their mountains and hungry valleys, they were all descendants of massacred Indigenous Peoples, their violated fore-mothers. They could hate the conquistadores for what they stole, but they couldn't deny they carried the same genetic particles that pushed the original invaders to wander into the unknown. Los es-pañoles occupied their land, christened it Nueva Granada. Diluted their bloodlines. Killed their tribes. The people they used to be. But instead, Mauro thought, they'd become something else. An adapted people unique to land reconceived by force as the New World; a singed species of birds without feathers who can still fly.

"Maybe," he once told Elena, "we are creatures of passage, meant to cross oceans just like the first infectors of our continent in order to take back what was taken."

Elena had more education than Mauro, but she let him believe his ideas were more important.

People say drugs and alcohol are the greatest and most per-suasive narcotics—the elements most likely to ruin a life. They're wrong. It's love.

THREE

The Bogotá of Elena's and Mauro's childhoods was another city from the one Talia knew. To the child, bombings and kidnappings were mostly faraway occurrences in guerrilla-occupied territories or distant campo villages, death tallies mere embers on news feeds. The hurricane of violence of the eighties and nineties was a specter in magazine retrospectives, horror written with near nostalgia, depicted on telenovelas. Nothing Talia, sheltered as she was, believed she needed to fear. In Bogotá, a girl of Talia's age could almost forget the terror, pretend it was happening in some other country across the continent, that the faces of the disappeared had nothing in common with her schoolmates' families, and the hardened expressions of children kidnapped or orphaned into fighting the nameless tentacled war could not have just as easily been hers.

Mauro and Elena's city of clouds was now a place where tourists came to dance and drink without the threat of death. The last broad-scale civilian-targeted bombing the capital had seen came the year before Talia was born, when their family was already on the northern continent, but her parents' generation was raised in a time when the Andean air tasted of gunfire. On the nightly news, in the morning papers, on sidewalks. Executions of presidential candidates, teachers, judges, journalists, elected officials, and so many innocents. Cars and buses loaded with half tons of dynamite, enough to take down a building. A siege of the Palace of Justice. Exploded airplanes. Entire barrios in shambles. Exterminations of the so-called desechables. Children stolen and forced to the front lines. Hundreds of thousands tortured, maimed, displaced. Massacres of police and of the poor—cartels, army, narco-guerrillas, and paramilitaries each trying to take down the other's loyal or purchased soldiers, and it was unclear who did the most killing.

Mauro was no criminal, and Elena was no saint, but Mauro felt they were unevenly matched in that Elena told him her secrets and he told her almost none of his.

Her life hadn't been easy, but since they met he had a sense he might corrupt Elena with the pain of his past, so he hid it from her, providing only essential components, enough so she could feel she understood him though he kept so much more opaque. To start, she believed Mauro had been raised in La Candelaria when the truth was he lived with his mother farther south in El Pesebre, a few blocks from Avenida Caracas in a small green apartment block with a slanted metal roof.

His father left soon after he was born. Sometimes Mauro's mother claimed abandonment. Other times she said she'd chased out her husband armed with scissors and a broom. He'd lost the family apartment in a card game, but she persuaded his opponent to forgive the debt. His mother had overlooked rumors that her husband had another woman and child in San Benito, but gambling away their home was too much to accept.

Mauro had his father's face. Something his mother never let him forget. When he was mischievous she blamed his genetics with disgust—esos ojos mentirosos, esa quijada de salvaje—throwing shoes at his back, shaving his head to cull his inheritance of curls. She locked Mauro in the closet for hours. Sometimes all night. She withheld food when she didn't want him in the house and brought men home who also felt free to push him around. People in the neighborhood called her la loca, but Mauro defended her the way he wished somebody would defend him.

The year Mauro turned ten was one of Colombia's bloodiest. It was also the year his mother decided he wasn't a good enough student to deserve to stay in school, what with the cost of uniforms and books, and sent him to live with her sister, Wilfreda, in the western sabana near Bojacá. To earn his keep, he was ordered to dig graves at a roadside cemetery with Wilfreda's companion, a limping ex-soldier named Tiberio.

They started in the morning when it was still dark. Marking grave lines for the day's freshly dead, stabbing soil with their shovels. Mauro hated his mother for shipping him off, forcing him into this kind of labor, but Tiberio explained it was safer out there in the sabana. He'd been in the army until discharged for a bullet in the thigh—a present from heaven, Tiberio proclaimed, otherwise he surely would have been killed in warfare like so many of his friends. "I used to be strong till they sent me to fight," Tiberio said. "Now look at me, half crippled and bald as the moon."

Tiberio also said most people only knew the Colombia of campo tears and urban shame, of funerals and outcry, of corruption and displacement. It was not the land the gods intended. The real Colombia, he insisted, was a thing of majesty beyond their valleys and cordilleras. There were jungles, snowcapped sierras, and black- and white-sand beaches on different ends of the country; rivers that nourished the Amazon, the life force of the Americas; cloud forests and altiplanos; the tabletop mountains of Chiribiquete, and La Guajira, where honeyed desert kissed the Caribbean Sea. Birds and beasts so powerful they could tatter this nation's most treacherous men with their claws and teeth.

According to Tiberio, Ancestral Knowledge said the jaguar was the original divine possessor of fire and tools for hunting, but the animal took pity on man when he stumbled upon him in the rain forest, wet, cold, and starving, and shared with the hairless two-legged creature its secrets for survival. Man repaid the jaguar by stealing its fire and hunting weapons so that the animal now depended solely on its physical strength and cunning. For this reason, the jaguar waited forever for a chance at revenge.

Tiberio had once seen a wild jaguar when his battalion was sent to patrol the Urabá coast, where mangroves met jungle. As one of the soldiers napped beneath a mango tree, a jaguar leaped from the brush to attack. They wondered: Did the animal know its prey was human? The soldier resisted, the jaguar disappeared into the forest, and the locals told him surviving a jaguar attack made him a magic man.

Mauro thought of this when he went back to Wilfreda's house that night as rain pecked the roof, and on many nights thereafter when, after years in the sabana, his mother let him return home. Though at fourteen, he looked even more like the man who'd caused her so much anguish, so she banished him again and, as he roamed public parks, struggling to catch sleep under the open sky, he considered how surviving a creature of sacred ferocity was enough to make a person holy.

Mauro went to live with different neighbors until each tired of him. He slept in empty lots and alleys, tunnels and caños, sometimes with other street kids who existed in a bazuco stupor until he met a mugger named Jairo who worked the streets of El Centro. Jairo took pity on Mauro and let him stay with his family in Ciudad Bolívar, the settlement built into cliffs on the southern cerros overlooking the city plateau, where rain turned dirt roads into gushing streams.

With his profits from robbing pedestrians and businessmen, Jairo had been able to move his family from a shack on the upper ridge to a house with brick walls and electricity on the lower edges. Mauro only entered or left the area in Jairo's company because the local pandilleros came after anyone they believed invading their turf. Everyone respected Jairo because he'd survived the police, who suspected he was in one of the barrio gangs when they captured him. They locked him in a room, stripped and beat him, pinched him with pliers, played at suffocating him with a plastic bag until he fainted. This went on for days, all to get Jairo to give up the names of gang leaders and their hideout locations. Jairo told the police nothing and eventually was released. Those were years when hundreds of teenage boys were murdered on the hills, victims of paramilitary hit men dressed as civilians, vigilante militias carrying out mass murders in the name of social cleansing. People said police only appeared on the bluffs to log the dead.

Nights, Mauro lay on a mat on the kitchen floor while Jairo and his family slept in the two other small rooms. He felt the tectonic pressure of the hills around him, each sunset walling him deeper into this unmothered and unfathered life. An impulse to run with nowhere to go.

When Jairo left the cerro each day to work the sidewalks near the Hotel Tequendama, Mauro went looking for a job of his own. He tried cafeterías, fast-food chains, and shops with no luck. He started hanging around the market at Paloquemao, trying to befriend vendors until he convinced an old man named Eliseo to let him stack his produce into neat pyramids at half pay if he let Mauro sleep in the stockroom.

Elena came to the market once a week. Mauro looked forward to helping her each time. She chose her fruit carefully while other customers purchased theirs and moved on to other stalls. Lulo and guanabana were her favorites, though she said her mother preferred maracuyá. Mauro packed them for her as if they were gems so she'd find no bruises when she set them into a bowl at home. She said she came all the way to Paloquemao, to this stall in particular, because they had the best selection. She thought Mauro's father should know and pointed to Eliseo.

"He's not my father. I just work here."

He was barely fifteen but somehow felt much older than Elena, who was fourteen, short and slight, almost feline with her long arms and bony hips. She dressed in bright pinks and flowery prints as if she lived by the sea and not their mountain city. Her long-lashed beetle-black eyes, often irritated from the detergents in her mother's lavandería. Hair pulled into a braid when other girls wore theirs loose so they could touch it all the time. Never jewelry except for her necklace with a gold medal of La Virgen del Carmen. He was self-conscious when he talked to her, making an effort never to use slang or show his ignorance since stopping school. He heard educated people speak on television and read newspapers that shoppers left at the market so he could have things to talk about the next time she came to his stall. He wanted so much for Elena to believe he was worth getting to know.

That April a car bomb detonated near Calle 93. The radio reported many dead and hundreds wounded. Bombazos were nothing new, but this time Mauro thought only of Elena. He didn't know where she lived. He imagined she could have been nearby. The area was full of shops and cafés. He pictured her hanging out with friends. Then the explosion, and all of them running to save their lives.

Mauro slept on a wooden pallet padded with cardboard, bunched under a cast-off blanket. Through the cold and humid nights, he often only managed to sleep with the help of liquor warming him from the inside. Tiberio once told him the Muisca believed night to be a time of regeneration, when the earth's energies were most tranquil. But the city was a song of police and ambulance sirens. He could not imagine what it would be like to sleep with silence—as distant a possibility as sharing a bed with Elena.

He counted the mornings until he might see her again. When she reappeared it was all he could do not to take her in his arms. Instead, he watched as she picked her fruit and told her he was happy to know she was safe.

They slowly went from strangers to acquaintances to friends who spent a few hours together each week. He traveled to her neighborhood. Brought her cattleyas from the flower vendors at the market and used the little money he had to invite her to a mango con limón or a cheesy arepa, which they'd eat together on a bench in a park or plaza. Elena always saved her crusts for pigeons. She said it wasn't their fault they were hungry.

"No," Mauro said. "It's none of our faults."

Months later, in December, Elena snuck him into her house, on the poorer margins of Chapinero, while her mother worked in the laundry on the ground floor. They slid through the side door, up the stairs, past the bedrooms to the flat and unshingled roof. The surrounding buildings were still low enough that the city unfolded before them among brown mountain cushions.

Elena never complained about the tedium of Bogotá's everlasting gray, its reputation as the rainiest capital in Latin America, a brume-billowed horizon and reluctant sun that only ever teased at warmth. Not even about the traffic, the noise, the rumble of tremors under their feet. Not the way Mauro did. He envied her for this, and for many other things too. She had a mother's love and the security of having lived in one home all her life, even if parts of the house were crumbling while every extra peso went to keeping the lavandería in business. He knew that in her mind, Elena had experienced a lonely childhood. No siblings. A father who left when she was a baby to work in Venezuela and never returned. Few friends beyond the people in her neighborhood, since most of her free time was spent helping her mother run the laundry shop. This solitude could be why she'd welcomed him so easily into her life. He was also jealous of her predisposition for forgiveness, counting herself fortunate, not forsaken. He compared it to his anger at the chaotic landscape, the city with its funereal sky, home to his mother, her back forever turned, tongue pointed in accusal.

How serene their Bogotá looked from up there, exhaled into rest after a long-held breath. Escobar had been killed on a Medellín rooftop a few days before and there was a confused electric current of ecstatic joy and hope that this would mark the end of the violence, tinged with disquiet for what might come next.

Mauro told Elena that Escobar was the perfect scapegoat for a country that was no better than he was. In showing his lack of conscience, he forced the population to confront its own. "Can any of us born of this land be certain we'd behave differently with that kind of money and power?" He remembered Jairo and the boys in Ciudad Bolívar gathered on the cliffs to drink and shine their guns, saying there was more honor in being a narcotraficante than a politician.

Elena only stared when Mauro said these things. He never told her about his years in the campo or in the hills, or even where he slept each night after he left her at her front door. She believed he went home to La Candelaria, where he claimed to live with an uncle. He'd told her he was an orphan, which didn't seem a complete untruth. Elena didn't ask many questions. She was not the way he was, perpetually looking back in time, sideways, thinking around everything. Elena saw only this moment, taking each day together as both their first and last on earth. For her, it was as if Mauro were born in the market at Paloquemao, as if the heavens put him there only for her. Maybe she didn't demand disclosure because she'd intuited all along, in the way he masked his restlessness, his default state of agitation when he was with her so that she wouldn't become wary of him. He wanted Elena to feel as safe with him as he felt with her. Maybe she perceived his need for sanctuary.

That afternoon, they sat on the edge of her roof taking in the coppery spread of the capital and its darkening mountains. He kissed her, her lips soft as petals. Held her hand as night swallowed the firmament. He remembered the sabana where he'd dug homes for the dead and thought of the betrayed and vengeful jaguar somewhere below their city, beyond anything they would ever see.

FOUR

Even after months, then years as a couple, Perla wouldn't allow Mauro to spend the night. Elena was raised on tales meant to keep daughters compliant. The child who talks back to their mother will have their tongue fall out. The child who raises their hand to a parent will see their fingers break off. One of Perla's most repeated was the tale of the elderly mother who asked her daughter for food because she was hungry. The daughter was cooking at the stove and opened the pot to let out its wonderful aroma but refused to serve any of it until her husband came home because, as the man of the house, he got to eat first. When the husband arrived and the daughter lifted the lid again, a snake emerged from a crack in the floor, knotting its body around the woman's throat, demanding to be fed or it would eat her face. And so the meal that the daughter had denied her mother was consumed by the snake, and the whole family went without.

Elena in love grew from an obedient daughter into an elaborate liar. She claimed to need to study to get out of her laundry shifts, taking Mauro into her bedroom while her mother worked in the shop below. Or when her mother was sleeping, when Perla believed

Mauro and Elena were at the movies or a party, they hid in the back of the lavandería, fooling around in piles of sheets customers left to be washed and folded. If there was enough money between them they indulged in a few hours of privacy in dingy love motels on the city outskirts, balmy in the bed, dreaming up a shared life. They wanted many children so no single child would experience the solitary childhood they'd each had.

Their first daughter, Karina, was born a few months into the new millennium. With Perla's approval, Mauro finally moved into Elena's bedroom, agonizing over the ways he might fail this child. He worried deceit ran through his blood, as dominant as his father's features, dark curls and arequipe skin, which he'd already passed on to the baby. He vowed to give her more than he'd been given. The only way to do that, he determined, was by leaving their land.

The end of the last century brought no closure to violence across the country, just new heads for the monster. From a populace rearranged by the dislocation of hundreds of thousands; to relentless attacks on citizens like the hijacking of a flight from Bucaramanga, its passengers abducted into the jungle; the mass kidnapping of parishioners from a church in Cali; the guerrilla takeover of the Amazon city of Mitú, where countless people were wounded and disappeared before the army response over three days of combat left hundreds of civilians, soldiers, and insurgents dead; paramilitary massacres in Macayepo and El Salado, where dozens, including children, were tortured, macheted, and murdered. In the capital, the No Más protests all but unheard by those who most needed to hear them.

"This country doesn't know it's dying," Mauro said as they watched the news after dinner.

"It's not the country we want, but it's the country we deserve," Perla answered while Elena remained quiet.

That much might be true, Mauro thought, but there was no law condemning a person to life in the nation of their birth. Not yet.

Perla's laundry was near bankruptcy since washing machines had become more affordable and most people no longer needed to send their clothes out to a lavado de ropa por libras. For a time, she looked for a tenant to take over the shop space, but the barrio building facades were covered in profane graffiti. During Perla's childhood, the street was as beautiful as an English country road, like the imitation Tudor and Victorian styles much of Chapinero was modeled on. Now it was a block most people avoided.

In those days, Mauro thought he would have to go abroad alone. He did not imagine Elena would be willing to leave her mother. When he told her his idea to find work in another country so he could send money back for her, Perla, and the baby—sustenance for the lavandería and to keep the house from dereliction—he promised it would be only for a few months. Then he would return, and just think what they could do with the money he made! How far it would reach when converted to pesos.

He was surprised Elena didn't argue, only listened. When he was through making his case, she pulled a tin box from under her bed, filled with crumpled bills. Her secret savings, she said, though she never knew for what until that moment.

"Take us with you."

FIVE

Spain was the logical first choice because of the common language. This was years before Colombia's entry to the Schengen Agreement that would allow them to travel there without visas, and so their applications were denied. Mauro and Elena decided to try for the United States, where they'd heard it was easier to get tourist visas as individuals rather than as a married couple. That's how they rationalized not having a wedding just yet. They told Perla that Mauro had a cousin in Texas who invited them to stay for a while. It would be a long vacation of sorts. They'd get to know the city, find temporary jobs, make some fat American dollars to pay off Perla's debts, and return home with their savings plumped. People did this kind of thing all the time.

In Houston, they quickly understood they were not guests but boarders, tenants. The man who took them in was not a cousin but a friend of a friend from the fruit market to whom they paid rent and who otherwise didn't want anything to do with them. Mauro found work moving furniture while Elena kept the house clean and washed and ironed the man's clothes. She would have cooked for him, too, but he padlocked the fridge and said they had to find their own meals elsewhere.

Neither Mauro nor Elena had ever seen the sea except in pictures and from the airplane from which they could only make out a desert of blue. A few weeks after their arrival, to ease her homesickness, Mauro fulfilled an old vow of showing Elena the ocean, taking them to the beach in a place called Bolivar, which seemed a promising omen. Elena had bought bathing suits for herself and Karina before leaving Colombia. The elastic pinched, but she didn't care. The sun had never tickled so much of her body.

They walked across the burning sand until the Gulf pooled at their waists. Mauro held Karina, gliding her toes across the current. Elena palmed the water. In her hands it was transparent, but around them it was all brown, tinted by silt and as murky as the Río Bogotá, nothing suggesting the turquoise waters Mauro had promised.

In Bogotá's interminable autumn, Elena's complexion blanched. In Texas she goldened, her hair feathered her temples, whipping with humidity around her neck and shoulders. At the request of his new boss, Mauro buzzed off his long hair, which sharpened his features as if by a blade. They sweated through their clothes those first weeks in Houston. At sea level for the first time in their lives, they underwent a metamorphosis, an inverted soroche of breathlessness, headaches, and ravenous hunger while their ears took in English, English, all the time English, and if they heard Spanish, it was with no accent like their own.

Phone calls to Perla were brief and expensive, so Elena tried to send a letter to her mother every week, though each one took days to write and weeks to arrive. She didn't want to tell her mother the mundane details of her life in the house while Mauro worked. The hours she spent pushing the baby in a secondhand stroller around a desolate park because the man they were staying with turned off the air-conditioning when he went out and didn't allow them to use the television or computer. She didn't want her mother to worry or ask what the point of going abroad was if one had to live in worse conditions than at home, so she filled her pages with commentary on the velvety warmth of the Houston summer, plum sunsets, and the luxury of so much daylight. She told Perla about Mauro's job, which earned him an hourly wage plus tips, since gringos loved to reward good service, and about people they met as if they were already dear friends, not single-encounter acquaintances they were likely never to see again. It was not the working vacation she imagined. She thought during Mauro's time off they'd explore the North American terrain they knew only from movies, but all Elena had seen, besides the day at the beach, were highways, roads, and bayous lining flatness upon flatness.

She wrote her letters at night, as Karina slept and Mauro listened to a small radio he bought, repeating words and sentences the newscaster said until they felt right on his tongue. At his job, he'd already picked up far more vocabulary than Elena. He tried to teach her some, but she didn't see the point in pushing herself since they would eventually go home.

They did not consider themselves immigrants. They never thought that far ahead and were young enough to believe none of their decisions were permanent. They saw themselves as travelers discovering new frontiers. Their visas were for six months, though issued at different times, so Mauro's would expire several weeks before Elena's. They'd had to purchase return tickets for January as a condition of their visas, but with the hours Elena spent alone with Karina every day, the date felt further and further away.

"I'm tired of this," she told Mauro one night when he returned from his job. "We're not seeing America. We're not doing anything here."

"I'm working every day for our survival and to send money back to your mother. You call that nothing?"

"Why don't we go home? We have a house to live in. We have the lavandería to run. I feel so alone here. We never should have left."

On nights when Mauro sat by the window drinking the cheapest liquor he could find, his back turned to Elena even as she called him to bed, she considered leaving without him. She could take the baby and return to her mother, the house in Chapinero, the barrio where everyone knew her name.

Things improved when Mauro found them a small apartment in Northside Village. A woman on the floor above paid Elena to watch her children while she went to work at a plastics plant. They monitored the calendar as weeks and then months passed and their visa expiration dates approached, debating whether to overstay or to return home. Elena was surprised it was now Mauro who was ready to go back. He was tired. The daily furniture hauling was becoming too much even for him. The men he worked with called him esqueleto, their own bodies thick from working in factories or fields. Compared to them he was skinny as a nail, more bone than muscle, limbs like arrows in leather sheaths. He resented the idea of becoming what some called *illegal*, as if just waking up another day in North America made a person a felon. He missed their city, knowing where they'd sleep each month, the fragrances of Perla's lavandería and the fruit stacks at Paloquemao. He even missed Bogotá's chaos, the city's brittle air in contrast to the strangling boa of Texas heat.

"Here we will always be foreigners," he told Elena. "We're Colombians. So is our daughter. It's where we belong."

Elena nodded. Their return seemed to be decided.

But then she said, "Mauro. I'm pregnant."

In Houston, Mauro worked with many men who'd navigated the southern borderlands by foot, some four or five times. They came from different nations, passing through the corridor of the Americas, sometimes intercepted and sent back to their countries within days while others were held for months in camps with no walls, only tarps shielding them from the prickly southwestern sun and frigid night. Still, they returned, even as the journey became harder, the hazards more vicious, convinced this land offered more than theirs had already taken from them. Mauro and Elena arrived under different circumstances, but Mauro knew the consequences were the same if they didn't leave when their visas expired. Without an adjustment or amnesty, a deportation order would come.

As Elena and the baby slept, Mauro held his family's three passports, running his fingers over the dates printed on each visa, Karina's baby photo pressed onto the page. They'd had it taken in a shop near the house in Chapinero. The storeowner droned that she was too tiny to go on a plane and it was unnatural to make an Andean child cross the sea so soon. He warned she'd acquire an incurable vertigo from breeching their altitude so early in life that would haunt her no matter where she went.

Later, Mauro and Elena laughed about the shopkeeper's insistence. But he wondered about the baby who was coming. Elena was sure it would be a boy. Mauro didn't know if she said so because she thought it was what he wanted or needed to hear, as if every man felt the primal urge to father a son. He thought of his own father who was no example to follow. Mauro worried he wouldn't have anything to teach a son about how to be a man but at least he could give him a life in a new land rather than tow him back to their pasts, even if it would cost them in ways they could not yet imagine.

At gatherings in the homes of Mauro's coworkers, when the men passed around beers or tequila, or when talking to people from the neighborhood, no matter their nation of origin, when asked why they came to this country and stayed they all said the same thing: more opportunity. For themselves, for their children, for their queridos back home whom they were able to support with money earned in the United States. It became true for Elena and Mauro too. What they earned in one week in Texas was more than what Mauro and Elena made in a month working at the market and her mother's laundry combined. Mauro had no education, and Elena didn't attend university because she was expecting Karina. With a devalued currency, theirs was a country where it felt impossible to get ahead if one wasn't born to a certain class, rich or corrupt, or talented and beautiful enough for fútbol or farándula.

If Mauro and Elena ignored the exit date stamped on their passports, the option of returning to the United States would be closed for at least five or ten years, at which point they *might* be able to apply for reentry. That they'd received visas in the first place, without American sponsors and with the quota on Colombians admitted to the country each year, had felt like the intervention of saints. If they stayed, they'd be limited to their existence in North America until it came to its inevitable conclusion. Unless one won the green card lottery, but they were too scared to apply to take the chance. Political asylum was just as elusive. Coming from a place that gringos regularly stereotyped as a death trap didn't mean they could prove they were unsafe without a documented history of threats. The perils of poverty didn't count, only a demonstrated danger of physical harm. Since they never received letters vowing to kill or dismember their families, they weren't deemed worthy of government protection. A good attorney might have been able to argue that even if one was not important enough to be a murder target it did not mean that person couldn't be killed at any second. But they didn't know how to find a trustworthy lawyer, having been warned about con-artists who preyed on people like them, self-proclaimed miracle workers promising citizenship in a year, who charged upfront, then vanished.

There also existed the possibility of Elena and Mauro seeking citizenship by each marrying other people, since they weren't already married to each other. The woman upstairs whose children Elena babysat had married a white Texan for this purpose. They only saw each other for appointments at the immigration office. She'd had to pay a few thousand already, and the rest was due in installments, but she never had to have sex with him and already had a green card in hand. The way she described it, marrying someone else as just a matter of paperwork didn't seem unreasonable to Elena, but Mauro refused to consider it.

They were careful. Scared even to play the radio too loud, not wanting to give anyone a reason to complain. They'd been told immigration officers only arrested people when tipped off. SWAT teams raiding apartment buildings, restaurant kitchens, or factories. Bulletproofed and body-armored officers with no-knock warrants, storming homes, breaking down doors if needed, as if the people inside were planning a bombing or a coup. They might take you away or if you were lucky, let you go with just a warning, but you'd be entered in their database, called for annual check-ins, and classified as deportable.

Mauro and Elena could always go home. Their old lives would wait for them. Yet staying under such conditions would prevent them from ever being able to visit Perla without losing the life they were beginning to make in the north. If they remained without adjusted status, they'd need to dissolve into the population, praying the laws changed, for amnesty or asylum.

Mauro passed time spinning bottles, flipping coins, pulling cards from a deck, searching for signs, a way to make the decision for his family to stay or to go. But there was no card for keeping Elena and her mother apart. No card for a life sentence of uncertainty. No card for forfeiting one country to bet on another. No card for regret.

• • •

Nando was much smaller than their daughter had been when she was born. Elena was sure it was the American diet, which somehow fattened a person while depriving them of nutrition. Mauro was in the room for the birth but was afraid to come back to see them in the hospital because he'd heard from neighbors of someone being arrested when visiting a dying relative, detained and swiftly deported. They heard such stories often. Mauro and Elena knew they would have to behave more perfectly than any natural-born citizen even if their complexions would always arouse suspicion. They were both people who followed the letter of the law, but once they overstayed they shuddered at the sight of police, who could ask point-blank for their government ID, and they'd have to admit they had none. For every deportation horror tale, there was another about someone receiving sudden amnesty, asylum, or a pardon so they could apply for residency, and they were filled with hope. And now they had a son who was different from them, with double the possibilities for his future.

Mauro took the morning off to bring Elena and Nando home from the hospital. He was about to leave them to try to make the afternoon shift when he got a call that the moving company's office had been raided. Mauro was sure the police would arrive at their door—having found his address in the company's files—and arrest and send them back to Colombia. Elena wanted to think him paranoid but in her exhaustion didn't argue, even as she worried that the baby was too small to be on the move and the stress could be dangerous for him. She watched Mauro pack everything they could carry, confused about why being returned to their country now felt like such an abysmal fate. They'd made the decision to stay in the United States together, prolonging their departure for the birth of their son, but they never said for how long. In her mind, it was only as long as the conditions were bearable. Now they were on a bus to another strange place, where another man, whom they knew only by name, a friend of one of their Houston neighbors, was willing to give them a place to stay.

Elena watched airplanes hit the World Trade Center from a Spartanburg motel room. The man who was to meet them at the bus station never appeared. Mauro took to the phone to call everyone he knew on the east coast to see if they had any idea where he and Elena might go, where they could live with their two babies, make a life, at least for a while.

She waved at Mauro, motioning to the TV screen. "It's not a movie. It's happening right *now*."

But his eyes were fixed on the paper in his lap, scribbled with names, places, and phone numbers.

As the second plane hit, Karina was tucked among bed pillows, and Nando, asleep in his mother's arms. Elena wondered if she was hallucinating.

Soon both towers collapsed in a ruffle of smoke. She thought of the water tumbling over the falls at Tequendama or Iguazú. For a moment she forgot she was not looking at one of the world's natural wonders but at a catastrophe of human design.

SIX

Talia was born on the coldest day of the year, Mauro and Elena's third winter in the new country though their equatorial blood was still not accustomed. They lived then on the edges of Hookford, a small and unfriendly Delaware town, after a year spent in South Carolina, where Mauro found work at a pet-food plant and saved enough to buy an old minivan from another worker. There, the family occupied a room in a barn converted to employee housing, its slats and roofing pocked and sagged by punishing summer rains. On the communal TV, they watched the United States shower bombs over Afghanistan. Mauro and Elena were born of domestic war but felt uneasy in a newly injured America, mourning its three thousand dead, so full of angst and vengeance.

In South Carolina they became used to stares, absorbing hisses from locals of *Go back to where you came from* while Mauro and Elena pretended not to understand. Sometimes when Mauro was out alone, someone would mutter *terrorist* at him, as if he were one of the hijackers whose faces plastered the news.

At a gas station, Mauro went inside to buy his Saturday Powerball ticket. Two starchy men followed him out to his car, walling him between their bodies and truck.

"Where you from?" one said, more accusation than question.

Mauro didn't respond, and the man grabbed him by the neck while the other punched him again and again. Mauro hit the ground, nose bloody, a tooth lost in the gravel. There were witnesses, though nobody said anything as the men sped off in their truck or made a move to help Mauro stand.

When the pet-food plant announced layoffs, there was an exodus to Georgia and Florida, where other workers said there were more factory and farming jobs. Mauro insisted the family go north instead. Elena wondered if even with their homegrown war, Colombia wouldn't be safer for them. But then Perla would remind her the latest peace negotiations with the guerrilla commanders had been a fiasco, and of the day of the new president's inauguration when an explosion killed fifteen near the presidential palace despite the high level of security; and the massacre in Bojayá, where hundreds of townspeople were murdered and wounded in a church beside a school, including dozens of children. Even the crucifix was left dismembered. It happened far away from the capital, all the way on the Pacific coast, but it was still *our country, our dead*, Elena thought. Tragic, almost, that she never felt more patriotic than when grieving her country's victims. The turn of the millennium showed no end to the violence. Elena knew in every war it was the innocents who paid, but in this American offensive, all foreigners could be perceived as the enemy.

Mauro spent most evenings in the common room with other workers, drinking beer they took turns buying for the group. Elena wanted to wait to talk to him when he was at least only half-drunk, but those moments were becoming rarer. She called him into their room. The children were asleep on the bed. Mauro and Elena sat shoulder to shoulder on the floor. Through the window, the misty phosphorescence of the factory lights. They'd already been given notice to be gone by the weekend.

"I'm tired of moving, always being strangers, having people look at us like we're a plague," Elena said. "We didn't come here for this kind of life. Let's go home."

She felt his beer breath warm on her face as he sighed. "We're young and healthy. If we don't spend these years trying to make a better future for our family, when will we? I'm not ready to give up."

"I miss my mother."

"Do you want to end up like her, spending your life in a house breaking down all around you? If we stay we can keep sending her money until she decides to join us here."

"We can sell the house and find another," Elena said. But they both knew Perla would never allow it, stubborn as she was. Even with her chemical asthma from decades of working in the laundry she refused to close.

"Please trust me, Elena. It's not yet time to go back."

In Delaware, on the drive to the hospital through streets cottoned with snow, Elena tried to find the seam between earth and sky, but there was none. Talia started pushing her way out hours before, but Elena wanted to wait until the baby was absolutely sure it was her moment. There was no time left for an epidural. She didn't have one when delivering her other children. Elena had only one ultrasound in the last nine months, early on at a clinic across the river in Blades that didn't require insurance and where she had to pay cash. They couldn't afford another, and she had no medical care beyond her instincts, but she didn't worry. In Texas she'd had plenty of scans and checkups, and the doctors were always telling her something was wrong with her baby, that she would be wise to terminate or he might be born dead or close to it. She didn't listen, and Nando was born small but perfect. Later she heard from other women who'd been told similar things and given birth to healthy babies too. She didn't know she would have a daughter until the baby was in the doctor's hands. With her previous births she'd bled like a slaughtered calf but not this time. The ease of Talia's arrival stunned everyone.

On the day of her birth, their home was a small bedroom in an apartment above a pizzeria whose ovens below kept them warm on days the radiator blew out, the scent of dough and cheese filling their walls. The apartment's true tenants were a couple from Pakistan. Mauro knew the husband from his janitor job at a local motel. He and his wife slept in the other bedroom and told Elena and Mauro to call them Mister and Madame. Mister worked as a front-desk attendant and Madame as a seamstress. Their teenage son died of leukemia years before, so his bedroom was empty and they sublet it to the family for one hundred dollars a week. Elena could only communicate with them in scrambled words and gestures. Mauro mostly took over with the English he'd learned at his jobs.

Nights were cold. The family wore their coats even to sleep, the children released from their blanket cocoons only for changing or to be fed. Karina was three. Nando, two. Madame looked after them so Mauro could stay in the hospital and hold the baby as Elena slept. She shared a room with another woman. The new mother of a boy. Elena noticed nobody came to visit them. She didn't speak Spanish, but when they were alone she brought the baby to Elena's bedside and they held each other's children until her boy cried and they traded back.

According to an American nurse who spoke Spanish, the woman and her son left the next morning in a taxi. Before the hospital discharged Elena, the same nurse came to speak to her. She stood by the bed and asked if her husband was around. When Elena said he'd gone home to check on the other babies, the nurse looked pleased.

"Now that you've got three little ones, you should think about not having more children," she said as Elena fed the baby from her breast. "There is a procedure you can have done here in the hospital to prevent you from finding yourself in the same situation again. You don't need your husband's consent."

The hospital people in Houston told Elena the same thing after Nando was born. For a time, she thought they might have sterilized her. She'd heard stories like that back in Colombia. Foreign-aid workers, Peace Corps, and NGOs. How they lured women to clinics offering free gynecological services and the women came out unaware they could no longer have children. When she discovered she was pregnant a third time, she felt a surge of relief that the Texas doctors had left her intact.

The nurse seemed frustrated when Elena said nothing in response. "I know your family is already struggling. How are you going to care for three children with just your husband's income when you don't have any other support?"

Elena was uneasy with how the nurse spoke of her babies as burdens. She never thought of them that way. In Colombia people said a baby arrives with a loaf of bread under its arm. Where four eat, so can five. Even Madame told her every baby brings luck to its family. She informed the nurse they lived with a nice couple who helped watch the children on nights when the pizzeria downstairs needed extra hands in the kitchen. The nurse nodded, and Elena assumed she understood they would manage.

When she and her baby were alone again, Elena held her and watched her sleep. This fat glowing child, pale from not having yet met the sun. They'd had many conversations in the months before her arrival. Elena promised she would protect her from harm and felt nudges from within letting her know the baby had heard. She'd made the same vows to her other children, and they lived shelled in happiness, playing in the back seats of the minivan, laughing even while hungry, making up songs for each other those nights they spent at highway rest stops before they found a new place to live, which she hoped would not be etched into memory.

The baby was named Talia for the actress who played the wife of Rocky. Mauro loved those movies, and Elena always thought the wife much tougher than the boxer. Only women knew the strength it took to love men through their evolution to who they thought they were supposed to be.

Mauro was never much of a fighter though. At least not with his fists. He found his corner in liquor when he came up against stronger, unbeatable opponents: a supervisor, a landlord, rent to be paid. The winter of Talia's birth, he drank as if it nourished his cells. When they were teenagers, Mauro and Elena went to parties where they gulped aguardiente and danced cumbia, shared beers and sipped wiskisitos at nightclubs and festivals when famous rockeros and salseros came to town. Mauro was the one who bragged he could drink more than anyone they knew and walk a straight line along the edge of a building. She saw him do it many times on the roof of her house in Chapinero. But now he was belly-bloated and clumsy. He bought cheaper alcohol every time because it was all he could afford without Elena noticing.

He drank at work sometimes, which got him fired more than once. At meals, even when Elena asked him to help by feeding one child so she could feed the other. But at the hospital after Talia was born, he promised, his head resting beside Elena's deflated abdomen, the child swaddled and asleep in the plastic basinet next to the bed, that he would never drink again. He'd found a church and knelt before an altar to Saint Jude, patron of the impossible, and begged for assistance in giving up the bottle.

"I want to be better," he told her. "The kind of father people remember for honorable reasons. The kind of father neither of us had."

He was the only man she'd ever been with, ever kissed. She knew Mauro had always seen her as a kind of seraph. It didn't bother her. Perla said it was normal for men to exalt the women they love. That's why so many had mistresses and why brothels were always busy. But Elena had the same desires as anyone else. When she met Mauro at Paloquemao—lean and long-haired, brows downturned in fatigue, in the moth-eaten ruana he wore till he saved enough to buy a flea market leather jacket—though he wasn't like the more educated or family-bred boys she knew, he had an elegance she could not explain. She remembered how she thought of him after their initial market encounters, the tide of love beginning to roll over her as she worked at the lavandería, hoping with every jangle of the door chain that the next customer would be him.

Since they came to the north, there were moments when Elena considered taking the children and leaving him. But she convinced herself every woman experiences the same temptation. Real love, her mother once told her, was proven only by endurance. Elena's impulse was always to stay, to remain a complete family. No matter where or how they lived, she was certain their chances of survival were better together than apart.

SEVEN

The landlord arrived unannounced. Weeks after Talia's birth someone anonymously reported seven people living in the apartment above the pizzeria when only two were on the lease. Mister and Madame tried to keep the landlord in the living room, but he made his way to the second bedroom and found Elena and the three children asleep on the pullout couch by the window overlooking the alley. Mauro was in the shower. There was only one bathroom for them all, and Mister and Madame asked the family to bathe within certain hours of the morning or night so as not to disrupt their routines. When Mauro emerged, dressed with hair damp, he found Karina and Nando crying. The baby, however, was silent, eyes following as her father and Mister and Madame tried to reason with the landlord, as if she knew before anyone how all this would turn out.

The landlord called it *unlawful occupancy*, because of the number of tenants and because three out of the family of five did not have permission to be in the country. He said he could not risk being fined by the city, that harboring "illegals" was some kind of crime, he suspected, though Mister and Madame insisted that wasn't true. He warned the couple that if they tried to hide the family in their home, he would change the lock on the door and have them evicted.

"You are good people," he told them. "Don't let yourselves be taken advantage of."

Elena didn't understand most of the conversation as it was being said. Mauro explained it later. How the landlord agreed to give them one week to find somewhere else to live before penalizing Mister and Madame. This was a special consideration, the landlord emphasized, because they had a newborn.

On his day off Mauro went to search for a place for the family to stay. He'd already asked his coworkers at the motel if they knew of anyone renting out an efficiency or a room or a trailer and came up with nothing. Next, he'd try the crew at the paper warehouse he used to sweep and then the factory where he once packed boxes of scented candles. They couldn't go back to spending nights in the car. Not in this cold. They'd coped before, in spring and summer months when they made their way up the coast from South Carolina looking for a place to settle, washing in gas station bathrooms. Elena spent hours in parks or shopping malls with the children while Mauro hunted for work.

Before leaving that morning, he kissed Elena and each of the children. The new baby was on her chest, Karina and Nando curled at her sides, still sleeping. Since Talia's birth, Mauro had kept his word. Not one finger of alcohol. Radiant with sobriety, he'd hold the baby, singing songs from their childhoods already fading from memory.

"I've had a premonition," he whispered, wreathed in muted light. "Better things are coming for our family. I feel it as certain as the sunrise."

In the bedroom long after he'd gone, Elena remembered the days when their love was new, taking hold like wildfire though safely contained by the mountains skirting their natal city; before they became infected by that dream more like a sickness, that their life in

Colombia was no longer good enough for them. That somehow, they deserved more.

If there was a time to return home, Elena thought, it was *now*, but in the past two weeks alone, a car bomb ignited at an elite social club frequented by government officials just blocks from the house in Chapinero, killing thirty-six, the deadliest attack the country had seen in years, and another bomb in Neiva targeting the president took sixteen lives. No country was safer than any other.

A woman was found dead in the dumpster in the lot behind the motel where Mauro and Mister worked. It happened the previous night as they slept. Elena watched the Spanish TV news after everyone left the apartment for the day. As with the bathroom, the family could only use the kitchen when Mister and Madame were not, which wasn't easy, since Madame spent her evenings cooking. Elena sat Karina and Nando at the kitchen table to eat canned noodles and held the baby close. The reporter said the victim was a motel guest, though the room wasn't registered in her name. She might have been a prostitute. It was known that many passed through. Businesspeople stayed at the nicer chain hotels up the highway. This motel was nobody's first choice. Mauro mopped the lobby and halls and bedroom messes too filthy for the motel maids to handle on their own. One of his coworkers must have found the woman's body. Elena thought about the dead woman all day as she waited for Mauro to return. She wondered about her family, those who loved her, if they lived in the United States or elsewhere. How sad, Elena thought, that her life's end had been discovered frozen among trash.

It was late. The children asleep. Mauro called from the police station. They got him, he said. He was in the minivan when two cops started knuckling the window.

Elena's first thought was of the dead woman at the motel. Maybe after finding out he worked there, they'd try to pin something on him. The hours in solitude before he called made her feel anything was possible.

"Were you drunk?"

"No. I promised you no more. I was thinking what to do about our situation, and I fell asleep. Just a nap. The car was parked. I wasn't in danger of hurting anyone."

Since they'd bought the car, they'd known there was increased exposure. But Mauro had never even been pulled over. He'd learned to drive from Tiberio with military precision and obeyed every traffic law as if he'd written it himself.

"How can they arrest you for sleeping?"

"They can do anything they want."

"Just tell me when you're getting out."

He said he'd passed the breath test but they arrested him for not having a valid license or insurance. There would be a hearing later. For now he needed her to ask Mister and Madame to lend them five hundred dollars so the police would let him go home.

Mauro reached out to a friend of a friend in New Jersey who said the family could stay with him for a while, and there were plenty of businesses hiring in the area. The police had impounded the car, so Mauro and Elena left the few pieces of furniture they owned to repay Mister and Madame their debt and took a bus to Newark. In those days there weren't border control agents patrolling bus stations like there are now. They sat the five of them in a row meant for two. Mauro held Nando and Karina, a child on each knee, while Elena held the baby. Dante met them at the station and took them to his home in East Orange. He was from Buenaventura and lived in a big house with his Honduran wife, Yamira, her son, and nine others; a mix of relatives, friends, and people like Mauro and Elena who had nowhere else to go. They let the family have the basement since the previous occupants had just left for jobs at a meat factory in New Paltz.

Yamira had a degree in economics but showed Elena how to clean houses. Elena asked what was so complicated about cleaning that it needed to be taught. She grew up working in a lavandería, and Perla kept their house as impeccable as a surgical ward. Elena couldn't leave her bedroom each morning without her bed made, clothes folded, floor swept, everything in its place. Yamira insisted cleaning for Americans was different and if Elena wanted to get jobs that could earn her a hundred dollars a day in the right neighborhood, she would have to learn to use their chemical products, operate an American-style iron and vacuum cleaner. She'd have to learn to clean fast, too, unless she was being paid by the hour, in which case she could draw some tasks out.

Elena accompanied Yamira on several jobs, watched how she made the beds, buried under mounds of thick comforters, and arranged the decorative pillows. Elena thought gringo households were full of unnecessary objects. Children had more toys than fit on their shelves. The wives' and daughters' closets overflowing with clothes and shoes. Husbands and sons with more cables and gadgets than a laboratory.

Yamira cleaned in towns with smooth, wide roads and neatly flowered hills, nothing like the twisty uneven roads in Bogotá. Her clients lived behind gates or in houses wrapped with porches like a ballerina's tutu. Sometimes clients were home as they cleaned, watching television, looking at the computer, or even napping as the women worked. Sometimes Elena and Yamira overheard conversations and arguments, babies crying with nobody to console them. Elena wanted to pick up those children, hold them close, but Yamira warned that employers preferred they remain invisible. Getting personal could get them fired.

When Mauro and Elena went to work, a woman who lived with her husband and two others in one of the upstairs bedrooms of Dante and Yamira's house looked after the children for twenty dollars. They managed this way for months, content in that windowless basement with the portable heater Yamira lent the family to keep by the bed where they slept in a nest of heartbeats.

Some evenings, Mauro and Dante went to a bar a few blocks away, where other guys from the neighborhood gathered. Mauro had started drinking again but much less than before, so Elena didn't bother him about it. He'd found a job in another factory. This one bottled hair spray in metal cans. It was under-the-table work, as usual, so sometimes the checks were smaller than expected, but they couldn't complain. They didn't have bank accounts. Every surplus dollar was wired home to Perla. When they were paid, if not in bills, they went to a check-cashing place on Central Avenue. That day, Mauro gave Dante his paycheck to cash while he ran another errand. When Dante later met him at the bar with the money, Mauro noticed bills missing.

Elena later heard from witnesses that Mauro tried to reason with him, but Dante denied taking any. *How dare you accuse me of being a thief when I've given your family a place to live? If it weren't for me, you'd be on the streets!* They said Dante pushed Mauro first. Petrified of being in trouble with the police again, Mauro stepped back, but Dante came at him with a punch, then a second and a third, until Mauro was on the floor. Some cops patrolling around the way heard about a fight and came to look. Dante was a citizen, so the police let him go without charges. But they looked up Mauro in the system and discovered his previous misdemeanor in Delaware, the hearing he skipped, his undocumented status, and took him away.

Elena was told only that Mauro was kept on an "immigration hold," then handed over to ICE, what used to be INS, who put him in detention. She believed he'd have to complete some penance, then be released to her. He might have to report to Immigration once a year like some people they knew, then they would be free to go about their lives undisturbed. She did not yet understand that Mauro would never be returned to them and was already marked for deportation.

EIGHT

At a café in Barichara, Talia watched tourists at tables hunched over guidebooks, staring into their phones, wearing leather and string necklaces, mochilas at their sides. They drank coffee and juice, connected to the Wi-Fi. The only Spanish Talia heard came from the television hanging above the bar counter. Among the hour's top stories: *a dozen girls escaped from a reform school in the mountains of Santander.* They didn't show pictures or give names, only reporting that four girls had already been located but another eight were still missing. Cut to Sister Susana standing in front of the guard gate, a microphone held to her face: "We are concerned for the girls' safety and hope anyone with information will do the right thing and contact us or the police. Their families have been notified and are very worried about them."

Talia was glad she'd swapped her prison sweatshirt for a T-shirt she'd seen hanging on a clothesline after the old man left her on the town fringe, but she still wore her school sweatpants, grubby from running and wear. She finished the soda she'd paid for with money he gave her before parting along with a bendición across the forehead as if he were a relative. She went to the café bathroom to wash her face, topknot her hair. When she came out, she saw a man had just sat at a table alone—maybe her father's age or a little younger, definitely not a local—and decided to approach.

"May I sit?"

He motioned with his hand to the empty chair opposite him. She'd learned a little English in school and from movies and TV programs that weren't already dubbed. When her mother put Karina and Nando on the phone, she was able to understand some of what they said, even if she could tell they spoke extra slow for her benefit.

"My name is Elena."

He studied her as if she might pick his pocket in plain view. None of the typical blitzed tourist expressions of dazed joy and overstimulation. She could tell in the past ten seconds he'd already determined he was much smarter than she was.

"What can I do for you?"

She understood he was waiting for lies so she opted for a version of the truth. "I ran away from my boarding school. I need to get back to Bogotá. My father is waiting for me. I have no money. Can you help me?"

He may not have believed her but was intrigued enough not to shoo her off as tourists do to children begging outside restaurants for change. His Spanish was good, though he gargled his r's rather than let them rest on his tongue and extended his vowels like some trench-coated villain. He said he was French. His name was Charles but he went by Carlos, since he'd been in Colombia for years already, obsessed with the country since he first heard about Ingrid Betancourt, held captive in the jungle, and kind of fell in love with her. He studied philosophy, worked a government job that was a slow eradication of his essence until he heeded his heart's call to South America.

Talia acted fascinated though she was already sick of the other café people eyeing her as if she were some baby puta looking to pick up.

"Do you mind if we go somewhere else to talk?"

The guy looked uncertain but followed her out of the café to the cobblestone road. He wore jeans and a T-shirt under a denim jacket. On his wrist, a macramé bracelet in the national colors, the kind Colombian girls give their foreign boyfriends.

"Where is your girlfriend?"

A look now as if this Elena girl had come to entertain him. "I left her in Caldas."

They settled onto a bench in front of a church on the plaza. He lit a cigarette and offered her one, which she took. Silence, until he slid his hand over hers. She was a virgin but had kissed four different boys since she turned thirteen. His hand was heavy and rough, but she didn't push it away.

"Tell me, Elena. What do you want from me?"

"I need to get back to Bogotá. My father is waiting for me."

"You just want bus fare?" He sounded disappointed.

She sensed he was a man yearning for purpose. If not for his whole life at least for that day. The sun was a buttery smear behind the mountainfold. In a few minutes, there would be no light.

"Do you have a car?"

"I do."

"You could drive me yourself. It would be safer than taking the bus alone. You wouldn't hurt me."

He hesitated, maybe expecting her to beg or offer something in exchange. "I don't like going on these roads at night. I rented an apartment here for the week. If your story is true I imagine you have nowhere else to stay. You can come with me, and I'll take you home in the morning."

She smiled thinly. "Can you also buy me some new clothes so I can change out of these dirty ones? I saw a store earlier. We can still make it before they close."

•   •   •

His apartment was one room of stucco walls under wooden beams. They sat on the sofa, a picnic of empanadas and chorizo between them. She wore the new jeans, blouse, and sweater he bought her. They couldn't find socks for sale, so he gave her a pair of his to wear with her prison sneakers, with their crusted canvas and gnashed soles. He'd wanted to take her to a restaurant for dinner. She explained that even though the news wouldn't show her face, her picture had probably been circulated among the police stations of the region. She didn't want to be spotted and turned over to the law when she was just trying to get home.

"Could I get in trouble for helping you hide?"

"They never do anything to foreigners. Besides, being charitable is not a crime."

He liked this answer and poured her more wine, which she'd barely been sipping.

"I can't believe you're only fifteen. I thought you were much older. Your face. Something . . . I don't know."

He was thirty-eight. He came to Colombia to teach French. His students were mostly rich Medellín housewives, since people looking for practicality usually chose to learn English. "So many people want to leave this country," he said. "I can't understand it. Why would anyone want to leave the most beautiful place on earth?"

Talia's father said people don't leave Colombia looking for money so much as looking for peace of mind. She told the Frenchman people left this country for the same reason he left his. It wasn't giving him what he needed. To that, he agreed, adding he always had the impression he'd been born in the wrong place. She wondered about that, if by birth one could already be out of step with destiny, but only replied that she was very tired and ready to sleep.

He told her to take the bed and he'd stay on the sofa. She approached the mattress, removing only her sneakers before slipping under the blanket, closing her eyes though the lights were still on. In the prison school, Talia lay on her bunk at night running films across her inner lids: images of her mother's face, scenes from her life in the north, a life that would soon be hers too. She knew Elena from photos, though she probably wouldn't have been able to pick her mother out of a crowd until recent years, when phone calls came with video—that is until the signal weakened and the picture froze or went black. On those video chats, Talia saw her mother's bedroom behind her. Watched as she walked around with the phone to show Talia their house, her brother's and sister's rooms. Elena said Talia would share a room with Karina when she arrived. They'd already gotten a bed for her. She took Talia on a tour of the surrounding land. Silken grass, trees with leaves that brightened and shed with the mystery of seasons, unlike in Bogotá where the only weather shifts were from wet to wetter. In her mother's winter, Talia saw tendrils of snow on their windows. In their summer, she saw her siblings sun-blushed, hair slick from swimming in the pool. Some days the Bogotá sun was naked enough for Talia to taste life beyond the elevated confines of the Tropics of Cancer and Capricorn, smashing the climatic monotony, but then the sun would cover in clouds again and she'd remember those minutes of summer were a lie. The best her measure of the Andes could offer was a cycle of seasons in a single day.

Some nights the story of Talia's family in North America crackled and faded as if she'd worn out the reel. On came memories of Perla; the years when the soapy scent of the lavandería filled her lungs, washing her mind and memories away with the rinse.

Talia first noticed her grandmother started calling her Elena. *I'm Talia, Abuela*, she would remind her gently, because Perla was a prideful woman. Perla also began to call Mauro the name of her absent husband, Joaquín, who was rumored to have been murdered

in Cúcuta on his way back to Bogotá a few years after he left for
Venezuela, but Perla never forgave him enough for it to feel true. She
was only in her fifties when her joints swelled—aging, it appeared
to Talia, at warp speed. Elena had wanted to bring Talia to live with
her many times over the years. When she was the age to start kindergarten, and each summer thereafter, to begin the new school year.
But Talia begged to be left with her grandmother, whose own visa
applications were repeatedly denied. Young as she was, Talia understood Perla would not survive without her. Being alone in her country with her family abroad would kill her quicker than the lavandería
miasma or the thin mountain air.

Those were years when Mauro was lost to drinking. Years when
Talia saw her father only through the doorway because he was too
drunk to be let inside. Years when, unwashed and disheveled, he
cried at the sight of his baby girl and only turned away after Perla
told him it wasn't right for his daughter to see him in that state.
When Perla became ill, Mauro returned for good. He announced he
was a new man. He'd seen God or the gods, had conversations with
angels and the ancestors. He'd been liberated of his vices and had
cast away all his torments. Talia was only eight, but she remembered
the vows he offered Elena over the phone as if in ceremony, to care
for both her mother and their youngest girl.

She heard the Frenchman's sudden movements. Felt his footsteps approaching the way she felt the nun's steps down the hall before she opened the dormitory door and Talia snared her with the
pillowcase. Now he was sitting on the mattress beside her. He asked
if it was okay if he touched her hair.

There were girls at the prison school who'd slept with many
boys and even grown men. They knew how to do all the things they
liked: maneuvers they said made men lose their capacity for reason,
bragging about it when out of the nuns' earshot.

She heard him say she was beautiful, though not in the usual way; she had *something*, an attractive quality, he said, and the jeans he bought looked good on her. He eased the elastic from her hair so it spread over the pillow, thumbing a loose strand from her cheek to her lips.

She thought of the girls on the mountain. People assumed her tough because she'd ended up among them. There were girls who were much stronger. They could have hurt her if they'd wanted. Her only defense was to behave as their equal, unafraid. What would one of those girls do in her place right now? She tried to summon their voices, but the best she could find was her own, faint but firm. "That's enough." Her eyes had yet to open, but her tone made him retract his hand, rise from the bed, and return to the sofa.

At some point in the night he came back to the bed as she slept. She woke to his bare groin next to her. Her clothing was unprobed and nothing hurt, so she was fairly certain he hadn't touched her. She pulled herself from the blanket and tried to step gently over the wooden floorboards so he wouldn't stir. She picked up the wallet he'd left on the table, examining its contents. A few plastic cards and some cash. His phone required a pass code. She wanted to call her father but had seen too many detective programs where police traced a number in seconds.

In the facility, the therapist pushed the girls to consider past decisions, how a single choice could have irreparable consequences. Talia understood this, but when she thought of the day in the alley by El Campín, she couldn't remember the moment when she decided she'd go to the kitchen and reach for a bowl of hot oil. The act took hold of her, as unconscious as breathing. Here in the Frenchman's apartment, however, she experienced at least a few seconds of deliberation before putting on her sneakers, grabbing his wallet and phone, edging out the door and down to the street.

NINE

Talia's first ride on a motorcycle. Its owner smelled of cigarettes with a touch of cheap cologne. He had smooth arms and a long scar above his beltline that disappeared beneath his shirt. Her thighs spread around his. Her arms circled his waist, and she knew he must have felt her breasts against his back. A peculiar closeness despite the noise of the motor, the heat of exhaust under her feet, wind burning her eyes so she had no choice but to shield her face with his shoulder.

She'd found him by the side of a narrow street back in Barichara after she left the French guy's apartment. The streets were quiet. She didn't want to take a chance waiting for a bus, especially when he might come looking for her after waking and realizing he'd been robbed. This guy was straddled over his bike, putting on his helmet, when Talia ran up to him and offered the Frenchman's phone and everything in his wallet if he could get her out of town.

He inspected the phone and counted all the cards in the wallet slits as if he received such propositions daily. She'd already removed the cash and stuffed it into the crotch of her underwear. He pointed to a government ID. "Can I have this too?"

"Everything."

"You shouldn't pick tourists' pockets. It will give the town a bad name. We depend on their money around here."

"It's not what you think. Take me out of here right now and I'll tell you more later."

He looked to be a few years older than Talia and not particularly dangerous. Unless he had a gun, but from her position as his passenger, she could feel every crease of his clothing, see down the seat of his jeans, and was pretty sure he wasn't armed.

The girls in the facility said if you are ever attacked or need to kill a guy but have no weapon, shove your fingers into his eye sockets and twist them like corkscrews. Don't be shaken if you take out an eyeball. Those things are not as well attached as one might think. Doing this will disable the guy so you can get in a kick to his scrotum. Once he's doubled over, grab his penis and pull, and when you have him on the ground like a dying roach you can reach for a rock or some other weighty object to drop on his head. This is assuming you don't have a knife. But if you do, it's best to try to gash the throat instead of aiming for the body because between ribs and fat and muscle, wounding to kill with a blade is a gamble you'd better not take. It's much more effective to bash his skull.

None of the girls were full-fledged murderers yet. Those kids were sent somewhere else, housed in a building with no prayer of escape. And should one get close to fleeing, they might be strangled or drowned in a bucket of water and have it labeled an accident or suicide. But some of the girls at the prison school were definite contenders for serious miscreant behavior. Not premeditated like a sicario, but potentially taking a life if sufficiently set off. A couple of girls had tried to kill their fathers, stepfathers, or uncles for molesting them, and who could blame them? One girl stabbed a teacher. She told Talia she couldn't stand sitting in that class, listening to that arrogant perra lecture for another minute. But as the girls said, *it's not easy to kill by knife*, so the teacher survived just fine, and the girl was sentenced to a year on the mountain.

The guy with the motorcycle didn't ask Talia her name. He'd been calling her niña since they met. He said his was Andrés but everyone called him Aguja. She checked his arms and neck for needle tracks to see if that was how he got such a gross nickname but they were clean.

He leaned his head back and asked how far she wanted to go. He could leave her at the gas station up ahead or drive a bit farther if she wanted.

"Keep going," she said.

"What's your final destination?"

"Bogotá."

"I can't take you that far, but I can probably get you to Barbosa."

They settled into the hum and pressure of the road. If she hadn't doused Horacio with cooking oil, it would be just another school day for Talia. She was a good student, but the classes at the prison school were dumbed down and she refined her skill of keeping an alert face while falling into a trance, imagining her life once she got out of the country. Going to a new American school. Speaking English. Enjoying life with her mother and siblings. She didn't tell any girls on the mountain she had a ticket to the United States waiting for her. They'd gotten to be friendly, but some were rageful enough to sabotage the escape plan out of spite. *Trust no one.* That's what her father always said. *Trust only family, if you've got family to trust.*

She didn't remember much about her early childhood. It only came into focus around age four or five, when her father began appearing at Perla's house more often, asking to see Talia. The rangy, sad-faced man, similar to the ones they found sleeping outside the doorway in the mornings before Perla opened the lavandería. Mauro always wore the same clothes and usually looked like he'd just woken up.

Long unwashed hair. Walnut skin chafed by the highland winds. Still, there was something handsome about him. She hadn't yet learned to be critical or judgmental. She looked at her father as a shining star, early inklings of what her mother might have seen in him when she loved him, before she let him go.

She remembers the day he showed up in new clothes, hair cut to his ears. Eyes bright and centered, not stray bullets shooting around the room like before. Perla let him into the living room, and they sat, the three of them, as if just introduced. Talia was seven that day, and Mauro made a big deal of it. He told her seven was a magic number and it would be the year that determined her destiny.

Perla said not to fill her mind with such nonsense. She didn't like that when they started spending time together, Mauro would share with Talia stories from the Knowledge about the origin of the world that contradicted Perla's imperial versions; that the first people were created not by God in the form of Adam and Eve or apes who learned to walk upright, but by the moon who put the earth into her vagina and gave birth to a son and a daughter. But even before the first humans, there was the darkness before light and the first beings the Creator, Chiminigagua, made were two black birds that spread wind from their beaks and from the wind came the breath of life that illuminated the world.

And that from the lake Iguaque, the great mother Bachué emerged holding a boy by the hand, and when the boy was grown she made him her husband and gave birth to his children, traveling the earth, leaving daughters and sons like stardust wherever they went. This was how the world was populated, Mauro said. Bachué and her husband educated their progenies, taught them the laws of humanity and the ceremonies to live and remember them by, and when they were old, they returned to the sapphire lake, transformed into snakes, and disappeared into the water.

Mauro appreciated that these stories offered explanations for his being, reminded him there was another land, a better one of divine logic wrapped inside this professed tierra de Colón, that he wasn't pacing the earth blind as he often felt and Creation provided clues that made paths clearer, as simple as the blackbird song that announces oncoming rain and the whistles of the Andean sparrow that signal the clouds will soon part. And also because they were stories his mother had learned from her parents before leaving their ancestral home in Guachetá to find work in the city, and were the only inheritance she'd left Mauro before pushing him to the streets.

Talia once saw a movie about a dead grandmother who visited her family members from the afterlife. She came to them each night, stood by their beds, and gave instructions and advice for how they should go on in the world of the living without her. When Perla started forgetting, her breath already something she could only hold steady with the help of plastic tubes up her nose, Talia told herself she didn't need to worry because her grandmother would still come see her after they buried her.

Mauro was living with them for a few years by then. Talia knew she would be safe with him. But she would miss Perla's face, her voice, the way she talked about Elena and Talia as if they were almost the same person so Talia could feel connected to her mother even though she had no memory of her touch or embrace.

But after Perla died, she never came to see Talia, even as Talia kept vigil and whispered her grandmother's name until she fell asleep. They celebrated a Mass for her in a church and Talia saved a space for Perla beside her in the pew. She set a plate for her at every meal and cleaned her room as if she might walk through the door at any moment. She recited Perla's favorite psalms, sang the songs she'd taught her, and when her grandmother didn't come, Talia sat before the large crucifix hanging in the foyer, staring up at the son of God—his glass eyes, that mane of real human hair—touching the five wounds the way Perla did every day before she left the house.

Mauro told Talia their Muisca ancestors believed the soul leaves the body at death and begins a long journey through gorges and valleys of golden and black soil, crossing wide rivers until it reaches the kingdom of the dead at the center of the earth, beginning a new immortal existence that's not so different from this mortal life in the upper world.

Talia concluded that her grandmother was still in transit, among the hordes of the world's newly dead, and if the traffic in the underworld was anything like rush hour in Bogotá, it would take her a long while to arrive. As soon as Perla sat down to rest, she would have time to visit her family.

Since there was no money for a cemetery plot with a proper tomb, Perla was cremated. Mauro sent the ashes to Elena in a package that was lost in the mail for three months before it arrived. During those months, Talia imagined her grandmother's ashes traveling the world, flying over oceans and jungles and deserts, seeing things they'd only seen on television, the world outside the barrio she'd hardly ever left.

Talia had no idea what her mother did with those ashes. She'd wanted to reserve a scoop for herself, but Mauro said it wasn't right to divide Perla's remains, and she belonged more to Elena than to either of them. But Talia thought it was wrong to parcel her away from Colombia, a country she said she'd never leave, even if the gringos granted her a visa, even if her daughter and grandchildren made lives elsewhere. Now what was left of her was already in New Jersey and Talia was the last of her family line in the Andes.

There was a girl at the prison school who called herself an espiritista, claiming she could cast spells and speak to the dead, and if a girl gave her their portion of dinner, she would cook up an hechizo or call upon whichever ancestor they wanted. She was fat from getting everyone's rice and potatoes, but most of the girls only wanted her to harm people they felt wronged by in life—relatives, rivals, the judges who sentenced them. One night Talia gave the girl her whole slab of pork, tough as plastic, but she would eat anything. Later, in their dormitory, Talia told the girl to bring Perla to talk to her. The girl closed her eyes, recited some nonsense words, and said Talia's grandmother would appear to her that night in her dreams.

It didn't happen. When Talia complained the next morning, the girl swore her grandmother *had* appeared to her, she just didn't remember it. "The memory of her visit will come to you in the future," the girl said. "Be patient."

If they'd been in the outside world, Talia might have smacked the girl. But since they were already locked up, all she could do was wait.

In the bathroom at a roadside restaurant near Oiba, Talia pulled some cash from her underwear. When she came out, she went to the counter and bought two sodas and empanadas. She found Aguja in the parking lot polishing the handlebars of his moto and gave him one of each.

He sipped from the can. The liquid turned his top lip orange. "You said you would tell me why you're in such a hurry once I got you out of Barichara."

"I have a flight to catch."

"Where to?"

"The United States."

"Why?"

"My mother lives there with my brother and sister. They're waiting for me."

"Aren't you afraid?"

"Of what?"

"Over there people walk into schools and buildings with weapons and kill everyone. They're not even guerrilla or paramilitary. Just regular people. What are you going to do when you're out shopping and some gringo points a machine gun at your forehead?"

"I don't think it's any worse than here. Just different."

"Do you have a father?"

"Yes. In Bogotá."

"What does he think about you going north?"

"He always knew I would. I'm American."

"You're lying."

"I was born there. My mother sent me here when I was a baby."

"Oh, you're one of *those*. Sent back like some DHL package."

"You're jealous I have a way out of here. Everyone is."

He gargled the last drops of his soda, kicking the empty can onto a patch of grass. Talia went to pick it up and drop it in the trash with her own can.

"Who's the guy you robbed?"

"Some pervert."

"Did he do something to you?"

"He tried."

"What were you doing in Barichara?"

"Seeing some of my country before I leave it." She was tired of his questions. "What about you? Are you in school?"

"Not for years. I do odd jobs. Deliveries when people ask. I used to work for a mechanic, but I got bored and stopped going."

"Who do you live with?"

"My girlfriend's family. I was outside their house when you found me."

"Lucky me."

"Don't start flirting with me. I told you I've got a girlfriend. You're a kid, and I'm not a pervert like that other guy."

"Who's flirting? I'm just saying I'm glad you got me out of that place."

He climbed onto his motorcycle, sliding his hips forward to make room for her. She eased onto the seat behind him, slid her hands around his waist, clasping them at his navel. "Don't get attached, niña. Just a little longer on this road and you're on your own."

TEN

When the police told Mauro his daughter had brutally assaulted a man, that she could have blinded him for life, he was sure she did it in self-defense. She never caused problems at home or school. She had the manners he never had. He was wrong. It wasn't self-defense, but still he believed she had her reasons and they must have been right and good.

In his meetings for addicts there was a lot of talk of being overtaken by the devil. They said he sent lesser demons to corrupt mankind in innocuous ways until a person found themselves trapped in a citadel of misdeeds. Some addicts in the room said they'd felt possessed when using, and one guy said that at his lowest, when he was selling himself for drugs, he found himself face-to-face with el diablo in the form of a client who laughed as the man knelt before him and said, *Look what I made you do.*

Some of their testimonies were hard to believe, even if in their country it seemed anything was possible. Many of the men were demobilized and reintegrated paras and guerrilleros with telltale awkwardness, agitation as if at any moment they might detonate. They never said so explicitly, but one could tell by their testimonies, which included hazing bordering on torture or being made to transport weapons and survey landmines; a life of discipline with comrades who replaced their families. Drugs and alcohol only came when they rejoined society, where they were shunned and their combat skills proved useless. In their old lives some might have been enemies— and often they were still hunted over old battle scores—but at the meetings, they assumed the tacit pledge to support one another's sobriety and anonymity.

The antidote to disgrace, according to even the atheists in the group, was humility and prayer. Mauro followed their instructions because they'd kept him clean for nearing a decade. But one day, when another addict started talking about the devil as some grand puppeteer, Mauro remembered when Perla warned him, as she was just starting to let him walk through her front door after years of trying, not to bring any dark energies with him because she'd already gone through the trouble of having the house cleansed of bad spirits. Perla wasn't worried about evil getting her at that late stage in her life; she'd done it, she said, to protect her grandchild.

When Perla became sick and Mauro moved into the house with her and Talia, when the old woman started talking to him like he could be her son for the first time in both their lives, Mauro asked her as they sipped tintos at the kitchen table if she'd been serious about the cleansing or if it was just a story to keep him in line. Perla had trouble breathing, but she often refused to use her oxygen. Not around Talia because she knew it upset her, but at night after the little girl had gone to sleep, when she and Mauro stayed up talking, she removed the tubes from her nose and pushed the barrel on wheels away from her side. "A lifetime at this altitude and now the air is too thin for me," she said. "What gives you life eventually takes it."

Mauro pressed Perla until she admitted that some years before, inexplicable things began happening around the house. During the brightest afternoon hours, the upstairs room, usually the most temperate, felt like an icebox. The water for the lavandería clotted with mire. She'd blamed the old plumbing and the unseasonal chill of winds blowing off the cordillera, but then things started falling from the walls—paintings, photographs—when no earthquakes had been reported. She found a basket of rusty razors on the doorstep, and Talia, who'd barely begun to speak sentences, told her abuela she saw silhouettes in her bedroom and felt them perch on the edge of her bed at night after she'd been tucked in for sleep. Perla called a nun she'd known since childhood, and the sister said the basket of razors was a clear sign of maleficio.

Then Talia came down with an unrelenting fever. Perla, too, began vomiting for days. On a night of rain, Perla ran around the house to make sure all the windows were closed and saw the immense crucifix she'd inherited from an aunt hanging on the foyer wall tremble and crash to the floor. The head of Christ broken off its neck, rolling to meet Perla at her feet.

Mauro laughed, saying that it sounded like a scene from a gringo horror film. The kind he and Elena sometimes watched in the United States, when they had a TV. Elena would cover her eyes with Mauro's shirtsleeve while he pointed out the ridiculousness of the movie. "Now I see where your daughter gets her sense of terror." But he knew with her story Perla meant that if he were to stay in the house with Talia after she was gone, he would have to understand the ways she'd cared for it and for her granddaughter. In this case, it involved a sort of exorcism, though Perla insisted they weren't supposed to call it that but a despojo of the highest order because the person who did the cleansing was not clergy but the famous former bruja from Antioquia who'd once advised politicians, casting hechizos that won elections and beauty pageants until she herself was exorcised and began working for God and the righteous instead.

The details, Perla said, were to remain private among those who were there. She could only tell Mauro that as Talia slept on the top floor, she watched as the ex-bruja moved about the living room, making the floor shake under a violent gust that unfurled through the house, coiling like a tornado, its pressure against their faces, until she instructed Perla to open a window and a vane of airstream pushed past them to the night sky.

The next morning, Talia was no longer hot with fever. She was calm and nuzzled into her grandmother in a way she never had before. But Perla remained vigilant. The dark spirits relinquished her house, but she wondered why they'd come to lay claim in the first place; if it was the ill will of someone she knew, as presented in the basket of razors, or simply bad luck, the sins of an ancestor for which they needed to repent.

Perla ran out of breath. It was more talking than she did most nights. Mauro helped her take up her oxygen again, and they sat in silence a while longer before she left for her bedroom. He never told Perla there were times when he wondered if he was the source of her family's misfortune. He was the one, after all, who'd taken her daughter from her home to that new, strange country and left her there. Maybe he'd brought the darkness with him when he was returned to Bogotá. Or maybe, he wondered, baby Talia brought it with her when she was sent to Colombia too.

A woman from the school in Santander called. "There's been an incident," she began, and Mauro imagined the worst things. He knew there were girls far more feral than Talia in that place. "Several of our pupils overpowered one of the guardians and managed to leave the property. Police are searching the area, but so far we have been able to recover only four of the missing twelve. Your daughter is not one of them."

She asked if Mauro had any idea of her whereabouts. He assured her he did not. But before hanging up, the woman said if he were to hear from Talia, he was required by law to inform the police and turn her over so she could complete her sentence, which would likely be extended due to her escape, along with possible additional charges since the recovered girls claimed the initial plan had been Talia's and she was the one who restrained the night guardian in order to flee. He couldn't help feeling proud of Talia's leadership and ingenuity but said yes, of course. If Talia appeared he'd call the authorities right away.

The woman on the phone must have known he was lying—what kind of parent would turn in a child?—because the next thing she said was, "If you don't, I must advise you that you, too, can be prosecuted in a court of law."

That night, the story of the breakout hit the news, a segment of less than a minute since there were more pressing concerns in the capital, like the hooded men who held up traffic for hours in protest of the guerrilla disarmament for the peace accord. The reporter spoke over aerial images of Talia's school and the land around it. Mauro pictured her running, running, as she'd never been able to do on Bogotá's congested streets. He said a prayer for her safety and watched the telephone all night waiting for her call.

The one who called instead was Elena. In the month or so since Talia had been sent away, she'd phoned many times, and he met her with different lies to keep his promise to Talia of protecting her mother's ignorance of her crime. Elena told him she'd called Talia's phone directly but it was turned off. Mauro couldn't say her cell was right there in a kitchen drawer, since she was forbidden from taking it to the prison school.

"You know reception is not very good around here," Mauro said, and started charging the phone so at least Elena would hear it ring and ring when she called, and leave messages. But then she would try Mauro again, asking why Talia was avoiding her calls, and he'd lie that she was out with friends, trying to spend as much time with them as possible before she left for the United States.

"Don't worry. I'll remind her she needs to call you back."

He couldn't help enjoying that Elena's frustration in not being able to reach Talia led them to speak more in the past few weeks than they had in years. He heard her voice and wanted to pretend she was only blocks away, calling to make plans to meet at one of the park benches they used to sit on as teenagers, so enthralled in each other's faces and touch that they didn't notice the first vapors of rain.

"How are you, Elena?" he asked one day after covering for Talia. "How are Karina and Nando?"

"Karina is doing excellent in school. Nando has a harder time but he's a good boy. They both help me with Lance."

"Who is Lance?"

"The boy I take care of."

How could the kid's name slip his mind? He heard Elena sigh and knew he'd disappointed her again. When they spoke, he felt she suffered through their dialogue. He almost wanted to hear her weep just to know she still felt something more. The last time he heard her voice wet with tears was when he was sent back to Colombia. When, after weeks of evasion, he called her and it was decided, though he no longer remembered exactly how, that Elena and the children would remain on the other side of the sea.

He'd like to be able to say he'd found absolution in the years he spent in the house helping care for Perla and Talia; when he managed to quit drinking and swore he'd throw himself off the roof if he ever let down his family again. Elena couldn't return to see her mother as her breath and memory left her. He knew that when Perla looked at Talia in her final days, she saw her own daughter. Talia knew it too. She was a compassionate girl who let her face become a window to the life Perla and Elena knew before anyone else came along. Each day that Mauro worked in the lavandería after Perla no longer could, he thought of Elena, hoping she'd see how far he'd come in his atonement and think him worthy of being hers again.

He wished he could tell Talia the things she never knew, things she was too young to remember, in case, once she left him, she never returned.

Before departing for Texas, Mauro took Elena and Karina, who was just a baby, on a day trip. Elena had seldom been beyond the city periphery. Mauro told her he wanted to show her a piece of their history before they left for who knew how long. For years, he'd wanted to see the sacred lake that Tiberio had told him about during his years digging graves, the place the Muisca believed the birthplace of human life. They had no car, so they took a bus. Karina cried and cried. He took the baby from Elena so she could look out the window, watch buildings turn to lush grassland pitted with cows. Karina went quiet, her small form against her father's chest. Her hair was growing in black and wavy. Her cheeks pinked, bundled so warmly she splayed like a star. Mauro had been the one to name her Karina. Neither Elena nor his first daughter knew it was a tribute to the mother who did not want him.

The bus left them at the base of Guatavita, where tourists and backpackers gathered. From there they made the hard climb up the hill path, Karina in his arms, to the mossy ridge where the shimmering lagoon came into view. He still remembered a calm unlike any he'd known before, not even in the sabana. Silence interrupted only by the conversation of birds. It was cold. Mist fell over them. He told Elena it was no wonder the Muisca venerated not only the water but the elusive sun, believing it to be much cleverer than the moon, more deserving of praise than even the Creator, Chiminigagua.

Elena had only heard the stories of the gold offerings the ancestors made to a lake long before Bolívar crossed the Andes. How, for centuries, greedy, thieving nations sent explorers and divers to Guatavita and to the Siecha Lakes to scavenge for gold, even attempting to drain them. She'd seen the treasures of El Dorado on a school excursion to the gold museum in the capital. Knowledge seized, converted to what they call *legend*, and made so famous it was like it didn't even belong to Colombia anymore. It made her sad they weren't able to keep their most beautiful things secret in order to protect them from the rest of the world.

The real reason Mauro brought his family to the supposed holy place: Tiberio had said the Muisca believed gold to be the sun's warmth and power incarnate; if a person harnessed it, one could make their own magic.

He told Elena they should turn their backs to the lake, holding in their hands an imaginary ball of sunlight, conjure their deepest desire, face the lake again, and blow their golden wishes to the water below.

His wish, to make a life for their family in the north with no need ever to return to what he believed was a forsaken land.

He suspects Elena wished for the opposite.

ELEVEN

Elena thought of destinies she and Mauro might have fulfilled if not for all the wrong turns. If he hadn't argued with Dante, had let him keep those extra dollars, considering it part of their rent for the basement that was a haven for their family.

Fifty dollars. A fortune to them then, but for Mauro, it was also a question of principle and pride. But was it really? Not when Elena considered what it cost them. Maybe Dante hadn't taken it. Maybe it was Mauro who had miscounted or misplaced it.

One of the alternate lives she imagined was if they'd never left Colombia. If their pull toward new frontiers had taken them only as far as another city. And seeing it was not as they hoped they could have returned to her mother's house, which Elena grew up believing was meant for her and the family she would one day have.

Would they have stayed together if Mauro had not been forced to leave?

Would he have stopped drinking for good and kept the family afloat?

All five of them. And maybe Talia wouldn't be the last child but an older sister to one more.

They could have lived in the house with Yamira and Dante a while longer until, with both their incomes, they would have saved enough for their own place. A small house with a yard for the children to play in. They were starting to build a community, and in that house of strangers found something like extended family. But from the day Mauro fought with Dante, even though the police would make *him* pay for the crime, Elena and the children were no longer welcome. If ICE showed up at the house to take Elena as a collateral arrest, Dante said it could endanger the other undocumented residents, who could then be taken too. It would be safer for everyone if she moved away. Yamira came down to the basement to tell Elena she'd tried everything to convince her husband otherwise, but he was so hardheaded, there was no point insisting. Especially because what Dante said was true. But she knew of shared houses that turned over tenants regularly up the parkway in Passaic County. She'd make a few calls and see if she could find a room for Elena and the children.

A few hours later Yamira reported that her sister knew of an available room in Sandy Hill. For now, they'd have to share it with another family until a space of their own opened up. It wouldn't be so bad, Yamira said. She and Dante had lived in a house like that when they first arrived in New Jersey from Arizona. There would be plenty of food and people to help look after the children until Mauro was released from detention and they were able to find something better.

Talia was still the quiet one who watched her mother as if she understood everything. At night, after her brother and sister fell asleep, Elena whispered her fears as she fed her. She'd stopped writing letters, but she and Perla spoke twice a month. She didn't say she was on her own, that she and the children shared a room with a Moldovan man, his Peruvian wife, and their infant daughter, deaf from birth. The two families slept on mattresses along opposite sides of the narrow cellar, the only clear space away from the boilers and loose wires, separated by a curtain of sheets. They could hear everything from the other side, but at least the material suggested privacy, even if a breeze of movement revealed the man slept naked, the child between her mother and the wall.

A summer night, after they'd all gone to bed, the Moldovan man pulled the sheet from where he lay on his family's mattress and stared at Elena, his wife and daughter rolled to their wall. Elena's children were asleep. She hardly slept though, and noticed the man didn't either, stirring and groaning through the night, often rising to pace the room. He watched her. Elena wondered why until he slid his free hand under his blanket and she detected the motions of masturbation. She hid herself with her blanket, turning to her own wall, sheltering her children with her body. Even as he moaned beside his wife and daughter, Elena did not scream at him for his obscenity, reasoning, however foolishly, that she didn't want to be responsible for causing hurt to another family.

Each night that followed, she made sure to cover up and face the wall, though she still sometimes heard his stifled gasps, and once, when his wife woke up and asked what was happening, Elena heard him tell her, "You're dreaming. Go back to sleep."

Elena's nightmares returned. They started when she was six years old but left her consciousness when she met Mauro. Since the eruption of the Nevado del Ruiz volcano, Elena had visions of her street and home flooded in mud and ash just as happened to Armero and the surrounding villages even though scientists said nothing like that could happen on the fault line of Bogotá. The tragedy happened only one week after the M-19 attacked the Palace of Justice, leaving more than a hundred dead or missing. Elena remembered the news images of the mudflow killing thousands upon thousands, turning the landscape into a sea of cadavers and torn limbs.

The socorristas saw a hand reaching from the debris, and discovered a girl plunged to her neck in earthen sludge. Divers went under and saw her legs locked beneath the roof of her house, held in place by the grip of her dead aunt. Survivors kept vigil as rescuers tried to figure out how to save her from the hardening mud without amputating her lower half. The girl, named Omayra Sánchez, spoke to journalists who filmed the brown water trickling into her mouth, her eyes blackening with each passing day, asking people to pray for her, telling her mother and brother through the TV cameras that she loved them. She was hopeful even as the country watched her dying on their screens.

In Elena's dreams, she, too, tried to pull Omayra to safety, but the girl felt heavy and only sank deeper into the mud, telling Elena to let her go. Other times, Elena became Omayra, feeling the weight of her aunt's clutches, her body tearing, her lower half sinking into what used to be her family home while rescuers pulled her arms and torso free, though she knew she wouldn't survive without the part of herself she left below.

People blamed the government for letting the girl die just like they'd let the people of Armero be suffocated by the lahars without warning they were in danger with enough time to flee. They said the military took too long to arrive with proper medical supplies, and they made the decision to let Omayra sink into the mud rather than bring equipment to amputate her legs. Others argued it was an impossible task. She would never have survived either way. Many said Omayra was an angel or a prophet sent to remind us of the ways we commit treason against our country and one another. That there had been signs if only people had been willing to see them.

The night before the eruption, the haloed moon smoldered red as an open sore, a divine alarm some would call it, Creation's indicator of an impending temblor. But others made excuses, said the moon fire was just pollution, urban fumes painting the sky.

In her dreams now, Elena was no longer the girl trying to save another girl, or the dying girl herself, but a bird or a cloud watching from above. The drowning towns, citizens reduced to parts floating on the carbon tide. Parents and children crying out for one another, so many of whom never found each other again, and some of the re-covered children adopted to foreign families in other countries and given new languages and new names. The impossible and unforgiving Andean volcanic chain. Elena could see it all from this distance.

TWELVE

Mauro was permitted visitors but only if they were "lawfully present" in the country. Elena couldn't even bring him a bag with clothes to take back with him on deportation day. If she did, the immigration officers might see she was undocumented and lock her up, too, leaving their children orphaned to the United States.

On their few calls during his months of detention, Mauro's voice changed. He became broken-breathed, throat gruff as if he'd spent the night screaming. But when Elena asked how they were treating him, he assured her it wasn't so bad in there; he met men who were doctors and lawyers and engineers in their countries, others who came to North America and built highways and roads and schools. Several were in detention for over a year already, hoping to be granted a "voluntary departure" instead of being branded with deportation. If so, they could apply to come back without having to wait five or ten years like Mauro would due to his arrests.

Some of the Puerto Rican guards spoke Spanish to the detainees, reporting news of the world like the August blackout that knocked out power across the northeast, paralyzing traffic and airports, though the detention center had a generator, so they only experienced a slash of darkness and a few flickers, a brief respite from the ceaseless fluorescence inside those walls.

Elena spent the day of the blackout on a folding chair out on the sidewalk with the other neighborhood mothers, while the kids twirled in the spray of an open hydrant. The men had already pulled meats from the freezer, and were grilling over coals out back. By nightfall, the power was restored, but the residents of the house acted as if it were a holiday, with music and dancing in the grassless yard. Elena sat with her children and watched, quietly celebrating that the Moldovan man and his family had recently moved out.

During the years Elena and Mauro contemplated staying in the country and the threat of being caught and sent back, they thought only of their lives lived here or lived there, not a fractured in-between. It never occurred to them their family could be split as if by an ax.

Elena knew Mauro wanted a life for his family in the United States, but they never discussed the possibility of that life continuing without him. He told her once through the buzzing detention center phone line, "You should stay. No matter what happens to me or what I say later. Stay." She pretended not to hear him. Instead, she told Mauro how fast the kids were growing. Karina was speaking in long, complicated sentences, making up stories for Nando as they sat by the window watching the street, telling her hermanito the pedestrians were magic people who at night ascended to the sky, danced across the stars, and trampolined off the moon. Nando listened, mesmerized, and Elena was grateful Karina somehow knew, at not even four years old, to entertain her brother so her mother could look after the baby.

Elena waited to hear Mauro's response but, as happened several times before without warning, the line went dead.

•   •   •

One night Elena dreamed they were back on the roof of Perla's house. She stood with Mauro and the three children under the aluminum sky, gossamer clouds pushed to the mountain crests, the church of Monserrate like a merengue atop its peak. In her dream, they'd never left their land. North America remained an unknown distant place. Mauro toed the roof's edge the way he did when they were younger, then took baby Talia in his arms. Elena told him to give her back, but he wouldn't, and instead held the child to the sky as Elena cried that he was going to let her fall. The next morning, she called the detention center and begged to speak with Mauro, but the woman on the other end told her he was already on a plane home.

Elena was not selfish enough to think her pain unique. The Sandy Hill house had several women tenants on their own—husbands and novios in other countries or held by the system. The neighborhood was full of mixed-status families. Sometimes they heard about Immigration raids in the area—sidewalk roundups or weekend sweeps at playgrounds and backyard parties—and people would try to avoid leaving their homes for weeks. With the apparent logic that removing fathers is the most efficient method for undoing a family, the officers targeted men more often than women.

Elena sat around the kitchen table with two other Colombianas, Carla and Norma, as the children played on the living room floor, with baby Talia lying on a play mat beside them. For weeks after Mauro left, Elena managed to work a handful of days helping other women who cleaned or at a bakery on Market Street. It wasn't hard to find someone to watch Karina or Nando, but even Toya, the Dominicana who ran a small day care out of her apartment, required that children left with her be out of diapers. Carla and Norma, with three children each, said there was only one way to manage. Send the baby to be cared for by her grandmother.

"She's American," Carla said. "You can bring her back later when you're more established. If you keep her with you now, you'll never get on your feet."

Going home was never an option for these women. When Elena brought up the possibility of packing up, taking the children to Colombia to be with their father and grandmother, Norma warned, "This is a chance you won't get again. Every woman who has ever gone back for the sake of keeping her family together regrets it. You are already here. So are your children. It's better to invest in this new life, because if you return to the old one, in the future your children may never forgive you."

What was it about this country that kept everyone hostage to its fantasy? The previous month, on its own soil, an American man went to his job at a plant and gunned down fourteen coworkers, and last spring alone there were four different school shootings. A nation at war with itself, yet people still spoke of it as some kind of paradise.

On certain autumnal days in the north, Elena could close her eyes and see the crystal sky over Bogotá, a blue that only existed at that altitude, the afternoon mountain cloud cascade when twilight swept the city in gold. She still struggled with the inertia of the North American lowlands, the feeling that she was always sinking.

She would have been happy living all her life in her country. There was an alegría inherent to Colombians, optimism even through tears, but never the kind of self-interrogation of "happiness" she observed in the north, the way people constantly asked themselves if they were content as if it were their main occupation in life. And what was happiness? Not selfish fulfillment, of this she was certain. That seemed like a recipe for the opposite. Joy was in the loving and caring of others. Carla and Norma understood this too. For them, happiness was a bet on the jackpot of a better future, a dream life that would justify every sacrifice. For them, there was no going back to the life before.

It had been Mauro's idea to leave. Elena only followed.

How odd that in the end it was he who returned home and she who stayed.

Mauro called Elena from Perla's house. He'd been living there since his repatriation, though Perla said he drank through most days and only left the room he once shared with Elena and Karina to go buy more liquor. Elena expected him to tell her to come home. Beg for it. She waited for his pleas, but they never came. Instead, he wept, "I failed you, I failed our family."

It was easy to keep silent through the erratic phone connection. Echoed voices and delays that regularly splintered the conversation. She couldn't tell if he wanted her to assure him, to forgive him, or to announce that she'd already booked a return to Bogotá for the whole family. Something in her hardened. She wasn't sure she wanted to go back anymore. She pictured Mauro in the house the way her mother described him, a ghost of a man, and wondered if she could do better for her children in the north until they figured out what came next, if there was a way to reunite.

She would look back on those months for years, trying to understand how she came to the decision. Was it a slow negotiation, or did it occur in a blaze of clarity or capriciousness? Was it the pressure of the women of the Sandy Hill house, who, in the isolation of motherhood, became something like sisters, or at least how she imagined sisters would be if she'd ever had one. She would recall how the homesickness that tortured her through her first years in the United States dulled and toughened her to the idea of going home. What followed was an accumulation of days that bridged one life in one country to a second life in another one. What Elena did not realize was the bridge had dissolved behind her.

She wonders even now, if somewhere in Talia's memory there is the hidden picture of the day her mother let her go.

Newark airport on a drizzly morning. The baby would travel with Gema, who Elena knew from the panadería on Market, and who, for two hundred dollars and with a letter of parental authorization, agreed to carry the baby on her lap for the flight to Bogotá and deliver her upon landing to Perla before going to stay with her own parents.

Elena packed a bag with clothes, diapers, and food. She'd stopped breastfeeding in preparation for the day. Since Mauro was sent away she'd worried the stress would make her lose her milk, but she never did. She found a bench near the window and sat with the baby alone, whispering in her ear that she was her love and her heart and they would say goodbye for now but the heavens would bring them back together soon. She used the same voice she used every day, one that soothed and anchored the baby's gaze to her own. But today it was as if the baby understood every word, because Elena had forced herself to be truthful, and the child cried as she never cried before, screams that turned the heads of passersby, and Elena cried with her.

She doubted her decision every day since, telling herself she never should have sent her baby away, even if Perla and Mauro both agreed it was the wisest thing. The price of being able to work to provide for the rest of the family was their estrangement. She wasn't foolish enough to believe that memories formed in infancy of being in her mother's arms could be enough to comfort her daughter through the years. She knew Talia must have felt the loss as Elena had or even more.

Some mornings Elena woke and pretended it was morning in Bogotá and their entire family would meet in the kitchen of the Chapinero house for breakfast before they went about their day. Other times, she woke and expected to see Talia sitting in front of the television with her brother and sister. When people assumed she had only two children because those were the only ones they saw, she always clarified that she had three. Her youngest, she said, was coming soon. And then she would have all her babies together again even if they were no longer babies but almost grown, and Elena wondered if it was wrong to pray as she did each night that her own children would never do as she did to Perla, leaving their mother behind.

THIRTEEN

When he lived out in the sabana, Tiberio told Mauro that in Chocó, Traditional Knowledge maintained that the first race of humans was extinguished by the gods because of their cannibalism. A second generation of humans transformed into the animals that now inhabit the earth. The third race of humans was created anew by the gods, formed from clay. We are only soil and water baked in the sun to dry, Tiberio had said. Is it any wonder we are so fragile and destined to break?

In his meetings, Mauro referred to them as his *lost years*. They began when the officers escorted him onto a flight in the early-morning darkness. He watched New York's rivers and light grid dying below. He thought of the candles with white dancing flames his mother would place in the apartment windows during the fiestas navideñas, the only time of year she did not seem to despise him.

When he found himself back among his mountains and stepped out of El Dorado airport, a free man for the first time in months, he saw the sky jawed with clouds and decided the first person he should look for was his old friend Jairo, the closest thing he'd ever had to a brother, at his usual posts on the streets near the Hotel Tequendama. When he didn't find him, he went back to Ciudad Bolívar, but Jairo's family had moved and the new tenants didn't know to where.

Mauro then went to one of their old cliff hangouts, where a group of young men spotted him climbing the cerro and surrounded him, guns pointed.

Mauro held his up his hands and told them he was there for Jairo the mugger. The group stepped back, lowering their weapons.

"Jairo has been dead for a long time," one guy said.

"Who got him?"

"Police. Who else?"

By the time Mauro arrived at Perla's house, he was already drunk on stolen aguardiente and it wasn't long before he vanished to the streets with his shame.

During his years with Elena, Mauro went from a boy who slept among crates in a cold warehouse to a man who slept with his prometida in a soft bed under a roof, a baby between them, to a father who took his family across the sea to uncertainty. He never imagined he'd once again sleep in parks and plazas until poked awake by police, taking cover from rain under flattened cardboard and chased out of alleys.

Every few weeks he would return to Perla's door. She fed him. Gave him a place to rest and wait out the rain, or money so he could go to one of those places in El Centro where they rented bunks by the night. Perla let him see the baby and hold her if he washed his hands many times and cleaned under his nails. Sometimes Perla convinced Mauro to lower to his knees so they could pray together before the Christ in the foyer and ask for mercy. He begged Perla not to let Elena know the state he was in, that he had destroyed their life together and was destroying it still.

Was it the disease or guilt that kept him on the streets, sometimes sleeping on the pavement across from Perla's house so he could watch the closed door knowing the baby was safe inside and that he hadn't returned to his country alone? He'd become unrecognizable to himself when he caught his reflection in shop windows, invisible to those he passed on the sidewalk with their averted eyes, shifting to avoid grazing his dirty clothes. He thinned from days spent walking, wandering, searching for places to sit, to rest, hunting in trash cans for food, engaging the charity of street vendors who sometimes offered a free meal. He remembered how Elena hated the northern winters. How they shivered and warmed each other, their children in their arms. How much colder he felt with nothing but fabric and skin to comfort him, wind knifing his joints and webbing his face.

As the baby grew, Mauro stayed close. Those were years when he and Elena rarely spoke. When she must have wondered if he'd died or at least found another woman. But he was close enough to watch the baby leave the house nested in the stroller every morning before Perla opened the lavandería and in the evenings after she closed. So delicate in how she rolled the child along, sidestepping bumps in the concrete that she never noticed Mauro huddled on the ground, draped in a blanket, shadowed in soot.

One day the child emerged walking, guided by her grandmother's hand in a pink coat, black curls peeking from her hood, wearing white booties smaller than his fists. He wanted to call after Perla, tell her the vagabundo they'd shuffled past had been him, but it'd been so long since he'd spoken, heard his own voice. He forgot his words.

He knew Talia didn't deserve a father like him. Pathetic. Contorted like some hooved creature. He thought of going to the Salto del Tequendama and launching himself over the waterfall like the Muiscas who, with all hope lost of being saved by Bochica, chose suicide over colonial enslavement. But the sight of this daughter growing each day beside her grandmother kept him alive.

Until one day when a woman found Mauro on the street and invited him to a shelter where she said they helped people like him.

He insisted he was a man with a family, not some lonesome crow moving through the world like a wraith. Or was he?

"You've lost your way," she said, as if it were so simple. "We can help you find it." Her name was Ximena. She was a few years out of university and killed by a drunk driver soon after they met.

Mauro decided if nothing else could make him quit alcohol, it would be Ximena's sudden death. But before she was taken from her living body, before Mauro arrived at his day of true surrender, he sat with her in an otherwise empty conference room at her organization's headquarters in the south of the city that reminded him of the stark detention center back in New Jersey where he'd met with court-appointed lawyers who proved useless.

"What do you feel when you drink?" she asked him.

"I feel her. I feel she's with me. I feel her love."

"Elena?"

By this time, Ximena knew all the names that mattered to him, how he and Elena left their land naive enough to think they'd never be separated, and that he watched his baby with the dedication of a kidnapper.

"No. Karina."

"Your eldest daughter."

"My mother."

In the shelter, he felt a corpse among corpses. Lizard-skinned. Dead as wood. They gave him a bed, a place to shower. Fresh clothes and new shoes. Potions to make him shit out his worms. He remembers the first weeks without the salve of alcohol, his bones rigid as irons. When he felt ready, he went to the market at Paloquemao to ask for his old job, but Eliseo was gone and there was nothing else available. The warehouse manager gave him a broom. Told him to start sweeping until something else opened up. Again he slept on wooden pallets, showering with the hose they used to rinse floors the way he did when he and Elena met. It was better than in the shelter, where he was surrounded by men who talked to themselves and who sometimes attacked one another in the darkness.

He began to visit Perla some evenings when he knew Talia was sleeping. Perla told him news of Elena, like that she'd found a good apartment for herself and the children, a job at an Italian restaurant. Mauro was jealous. He imagined men falling in love with her. How could they not when she was so beautiful, tender, and kind? In Texas, she'd mentioned the possibility of marrying another man so she could get her papers. The idea still made him feel ill. In his absence, he knew it was an even more attractive solution. Mauro feared Elena would replace him and that Karina and Nando could soon call another man their father.

FOURTEEN

Elena found a job mopping and cleaning bathrooms in a restaurant a few towns over. The owner was young, spoke Spanish learned while surfing in Nicaragua, and was pleasant except that he didn't pay Elena for her first month on the job, saying it was customary to work for free during the "trial period." She asked the guys in the kitchen if this was true, but they wouldn't say. One month without income indebted her to many others. With a loan from Carla she was able to pay for the basement in the Sandy Hill house and Lety, who cooked meals for residents who contributed to the grocery bills, let Elena and the kids eat on credit.

That night: white-breath cold, shop windows scalloped in frost, the town tinseled for the holidays. The restaurant closed to the public for a private party. At the end of the shift, after Elena did her final wiping-downs and pushed her buckets into the supply closet, she gathered her things from her locker and heard the boss call her from his office. She held her coat and handbag against her stomach and followed his voice. Before she could ask if something was wrong he shut the door behind her, closed the space between them, swishing his tongue in her mouth. She tasted alcohol, moved back, but he swept the coat and bag from her hands and pushed her against the wall. He spoke in English she didn't understand, lifting her shirt, tugging her bra so the strap carved into her shoulder and her breasts fell out. He pinched and bit as she pushed him away, sailed her shirt over her head blinding her, angled her to the desk, pants at her knees, and tore into her from behind. Elena. Small, birdlike, as Mauro used to say, who brought three children into the world, shocked into pain far beyond the flesh.

Grunting until his final spasms. She still cannot say how much time passed. Minutes maybe, but she was already gone, soul departed, searching for remnants of who she'd been just minutes before. When he removed himself from her, she felt him cover her back with her coat. She pulled up her pants, her stretched underwear. She managed to ask why.

Without meeting her eyes he said, "I don't know. I'm not usually attracted to mothers."

She walked to the bus stop, scalp burning from where he pulled, propped onto her hip the whole ride because it hurt too much to sit, weeping into her sleeve. The next morning, when she went to pick up the children from Toya's, she told her what happened as plainly as she could. Toya had been in the United States much longer, and Elena hoped she'd have some advice or wisdom. She heard her own voice as if it belonged to someone else. Toya walked to her stove, turned the heat on under the kettle, and leaned against the counter.

"Amiga, I'm sorry to say these things happen all the time. Try to forget it."

"What do I do about the boss?"

"Nothing. You can't report him. The police won't believe you. They could ask for your papers and arrest you because you don't have any. They'll send you back to your country and split up the kids because Nando was born here and Karina wasn't. Go back to work and get your money. Start wearing a wedding ring. Don't be alone with him. And if he tries again, remember it will soon be over."

If she'd spoken to anyone but Toya that day, she might have gone about things differently. But Elena trusted her to watch her children, and so she trusted her counsel too. She decided never to speak again of what happened in the restaurant even if she relived it in her mind without end. Not to Mauro, to Perla, to anyone. Instead, she lit a candle every night to the devotional card of the Virgen de Chiquinquirá her mother gave her before leaving for the United States. She begged not to become pregnant and cried when her period finally came.

It was Talia's first Christmas and Elena's first without Mauro since they'd met. The restaurant gave bonuses for the holidays. Elena was able to buy toys for Nando and Karina. She sent the rest to Perla to buy something for the baby and set some apart for Mauro for when he turned up at the house.

Her calls with Perla got shorter. She couldn't bear to lie to her mother, tell her everything was all right when it wasn't. Normally Perla would put the baby on the phone before hanging up, but Elena was afraid of passing her pain to the child, as if contagious even by sound. She felt a liar, a conspirator to the man who abused her because she protected him with silence. Now she understood why he chose her.

Elena and the children celebrated Nochebuena with the other residents of the Sandy Hill house who'd all pitched in to buy a Christmas tree, decorated with homemade ornaments and paper garlands, and between them prepared a feast. They'd just finished eating when Elena's phone rang. She heard Mauro's faint voice, his first call in months.

"It sounds like a great party."

Elena ached to confess that despite the guitar strums and villancicos he heard sung in the background, she was drowning without him, but she knew in his own way he was drowning too. She put the children on the phone so they could hear their father and imagined the things he might be saying to them, watching their expressions of glee and confusion. *Papi*, they said over and over. *Es Papi*.

Elena remembered a story Perla told her in the months before she and Mauro left Colombia. They were sweeping the lavandería as they did every evening after locking up. Elena worried about leaving her mother alone. The workers they hired were undependable, rarely lasting more than a few weeks. Perla told her about a mother and daughter who lived alone together like they had before Elena met Mauro. The mother and daughter were very close, loved each other very much, and had no family but each other. One day they were walking together on the road when they were confronted by a wicked man who macheted them both to death. The daughter had lived a pure life, so she went straight to heaven. But the mother had lived a longer, more complicated life, so she waited in limbo, looking up to heaven, and one day spotted her daughter in all her eternal glory. She called for her daughter to lower her hair so she could climb it and join her in the upper world. The daughter dropped her braids, her mother climbed, and the two were overjoyed at being reunited. The mother thought her daughter had saved her from languishing in the void, Perla had said. She didn't know she'd already been purified, that her daughter was only waiting until it was the mother's turn to be called home.

FIFTEEN

Mauro's sobriety was still a fragile thing. He sometimes squandered months of it for a few blurry days that would leave him feeling sick down to his liver. He didn't yet feel ready to return to live with Talia and Perla but visited often, and saw that in his daughter's eyes he was becoming more familiar, someone she looked at with delight. He no longer resembled those she called "outside people," who wiped windshields at intersections, or the unsheltered day-sleepers on sidewalks and patches of dead grass. Sometimes he brought Talia flowers, which she'd pull apart petal by petal, or a peluche when he could afford it. Her favorite was a small yellow bear that she took everywhere until she dropped it during an outing with her grandmother. At least that's what Perla told him. He brought her a pink bear as a replacement, but she didn't love it in the same way.

In one of his meetings Mauro met a man who asked if he did handiwork. He said he managed an apartment building near El Retiro. They were looking for someone to do maintenance and repairs around the property.

Mauro appeared at Perla's door in a new uniform, said he had a good job and was ready to live in the house again, that he could pay more than his share and help with the lavandería before and after his shifts. He saw how Perla was struggling. Fewer customers and other supposedly loyal ones who never paid their long-running tabs. Perla was becoming sick too. Her breathing laborious, coughing fits that produced dots of blood. But she refused to see a doctor. Mauro, not wanting to disrespect her, didn't insist.

Mauro and Elena spoke every few weeks, mostly because she was calling for Perla and he happened to answer. Conversations that were largely transactional. He reported on the lavandería, told her what Perla wouldn't, like that they'd moved her bed to the room on the ground floor behind the kitchen because the stairs overwhelmed her. Her memory fragmenting, words and names for things slipping from her grasp; how she referred to Karina and Nando as *the girl* and *the boy* and one day, when Mauro asked Perla to say their names, she could not.

Mauro told Elena that Perla's memory was restored in Talia's presence. She knew every detail of her granddaughter's life. The way she liked each meal prepared down to the stirring of a spice, waking to dress her for school, watching as she left the house with Mauro, who dropped her at class on his way to work. For Talia, her grandmother was not a fading sunset but a woman burning bright. And so, Elena agreed to postpone sending for her daughter to join her in the United States knowing, as Mauro did, that Perla would not survive long without her.

In the years that Mauro drifted further from the life he had with Elena, Karina, and Nando, he rooted deeper into his life with Talia. He heard his other children's resistance when Elena forced them to the phone with him. Monosyllabic. They no longer called him Papi or Papá but Dad or nothing at all. He could not deny Talia was special to him because she was the one he watched grow.

When she was seven, Mauro took her to the lake. It was the first time Perla let him travel beyond the barrio with the child without supervision. They took the bus across city limits, and Mauro carried her up the mountain slope on his back.

He told her about Bochica, the Muisca god of wisdom who taught laws and morals to his people, and his rival, Chibchacum, who punished the world with the ancient diluvio, a universal flood that submerged all life until, with his staff, Bochica forced sunrays through the rain clouds, and the water puddled and parted, making lakes and fertile valleys, pushing the excess through the mountain belt into what became the Tequendama waterfalls. Mauro told Talia how Bochica sentenced Chibchacum to carry the world on his back, and every time they felt an earthquake, it was just Chibchacum shifting under the weight.

When they reached the top, taking in the valley of water below, Talia asked why they couldn't go swimming in it. Mauro said Guatavita was a sacred lake. They'd come to honor it, and he'd been there with her mother and sister to make wishes for their new life in the north. He told her what Tiberio once told him: When the world was new, the creatures that ruled were the jaguar, the snake, and the condor. Of the snakes, the anaconda, the most massive serpent, swam in jungle waters among fish with tails as long as rainbows, crabs and turtles as wide as cars, crocodiles four times the size of the dwarfed ones that dwell in the Amazon and Orinoco Rivers. The boa queen was above all predators, able to constrict the life out of any creature she wanted. The boa's power was its silence; eyes that saw everything, movement so graceful and subtle that no other animal could sense they were being watched or hunted. The snake didn't need to prove its danger. The snake knew power came from patience.

Mauro told Talia about the serpent that lived at the bottom of the lagoon. Some said she was Bachué, mother of the Muisca. Others insisted the serpent was the devil.

From the lake we came and to the lake we will return, Mauro repeated Tiberio's words, though Talia's eyes were on the birds circling above. *We're all migrants here on earth.*

There was one story of Guatavita Mauro never told Elena or either of his daughters when he took them to see the lake. A story he wished he'd never learned, though it came from his mother, and was one he'd never be able to forget.

The territory surrounding the lake was once governed by a powerful cacique who was married to a princess from another tribe and with whom he had a daughter. But the cacique was often drunk on chicha, off at bacchanals, and in his absence, his wife fell in love with a young warrior. The lovers were caught, and the cacique had the warrior tortured, cut out his heart, and presented it to his wife as proof of his ruthlessness and her infidelity. The princess ran away, thrusting herself, with her daughter in her arms, into the lake. The cacique sent his high priests to search for them. They soon returned to inform the cacique that his wife now lived below in the water kingdom as the bride of an enormous serpent. The cacique demanded his daughter be returned to him. The serpent sent back a young girl who resembled his daughter but with her eyes removed, so she could not see her father, recoiling when he tried to embrace her. And so it was the cacique who submitted, returning his beloved daughter to the lake to live with her mother and the serpent until the end of time.

SIXTEEN

Before they left for Texas, people warned Elena everyone gets fat in the north. Chemicals replace natural ingredients, so bread is not bread by the time one eats it. Meat from hormone-reared animals, mutant produce, colorful and rotund yet flavorless. Where fresh was expensive, and cheap was a tasty poison packaged as a meal. But after each time she gave birth in the United States, her body restored itself to its original form. It was after Mauro left that her body became something else, even as she walked more, ate less, carrying the children and their belongings every time they moved. She was stronger but never felt more tired or shapeless. When cell phones enabled people to see the person on the other side of the call, Elena held the camera close to her face to conceal from Mauro her new bulges.

She remembered the first time Mauro's eyes glinted in that small screen. For years she'd imagined them meeting again, and there he was in her hand, gaunt, his forehead wide and square. The long hair she so loved to bury her face in was gone. She could tell he was taking in the sight of her too. The new wrinkles mapping old smiles, grays sparking from her temples.

"You're as beautiful as ever, Elena."

"I'm not and I know it. You don't have to lie."

Silence anchored until Talia took the phone from her father to ask Elena to send money to buy a new schoolbag.

"The one you have is perfectly fine," Mauro said, and Talia argued briefly as Elena watched through the phone, a spectator to an intimacy she no longer shared with either of them.

Perhaps it had nothing to do with her body but with what the man at the restaurant did to her. The only man she'd ever been with besides Mauro. Their separation was involuntary. But time and borders did more to distance them than any divorce or widowing could.

She'd remained faithful. If not with her body, with her mind and heart, still with Mauro even through his years lost to drinking and hiding in city streets, despite the sporadic contact and stilted conversations, the silence that on her end, at least, held fear that it would be that way forever. She had many nightmares, but when her dreams were good, they were only of him, of being old with Mauro, their children safe and grown with families of their own. In her dreams they were always back in Colombia, never in the north, waiting peacefully for death to find them in their own land.

She stayed to work at the restaurant a few months longer. These were zombie days of obstinate nausea when Elena understood that what she said or wanted meant nothing. She kept what happened to herself, even when she'd hear about another woman from the neighborhood who went through something similar. They never commiserated. They kept each other strong so they could keep mothering and survive.

Maybe it goes back to the first time she got paid in the United States, apart from Mauro's income, and was able to send money back to her mother. A pride, a satisfaction like no other she'd known. To be able to give to the one who gave her everything. To be able to make Perla's days easier. A feeling that brought meaning and light to every dark day that came before or after.

One spring day with a morning moon, instead of walking from the bus stop to her regular shift at the restaurant, Elena turned and headed past the main avenue to streets lined with houses, expensive cars parked in driveways, and began knocking on doors. In her best English, she pronounced: *I can clean your house. First time you pay what you want.*

She soon had a few regular clients. She tried to be discerning. Yamira had taught her to be careful for whom she cleaned. Just like at any other job, one could be assaulted by an employer or work for weeks without getting paid.

Some houses were bigger than others. In one case, the current housekeeper had just been fired. In another, the lady of the house told Elena her husband demanded she do the cleaning herself but she would hire her if she promised not to tell anyone and be gone before the husband returned from work. In another home, the patrona made Elena wear slipcovers over her shoes. In another, no shoes were permitted at all. One man insisted Elena clean everything with bleach, which made her so dizzy she'd often have to lie on the bathroom floor, cheek to tile, until she could see clearly again. Some nights, she coughed through her sleep. Hands calloused, fingertips inflamed. Back sore and feet blistered from treks to each house to the bus station and back home. But the money. It was everything.

From her cleaning pay, she was able to set some aside to pay a lawyer she found through Toya to help her apply for a green card. He asked for only five hundred up front and collected the rest in monthly installments, which she could save by washing and folding clothes for other residents of the Sandy Hill house at the coin laundry. But after nearly a year of payments and nothing to show for them, Elena went to the lawyer's office to inquire about her case's progress and found his office had been vacated.

She cleaned the house of a woman who learned Spanish during a school exchange in Sevilla. She loved to practice and sometimes invited Elena to sit with her as she ate lunch. She told her about the boyfriend she had in Spain who she still thought about, found on the internet, and dreamed of contacting. Elena felt she could trust this woman the way she trusted her. She told her what happened with the lawyer, hoping she might have advice since she was married to a lawyer, though her husband worked at a bank. She explained the family's situation, how Mauro had been sent back. It was the first time she'd ever gotten so personal with a boss, but this woman struck Elena as compassionate, how she straightened her house before Elena arrived to clean and always apologized for her son's messes. She was surprised to learn Elena had three children, since she'd never mentioned them, including a boy exactly her own son's age.

"Can I ask you a question?" the woman said.

Elena thought it would be something about Mauro's case. Maybe his deportation story sounded too far-fetched.

"Why do your people have so many children when you can't afford to take care of them?"

The way she said *your people*—gente como tú—with a biting gringa twang, confused Elena, since she thought of herself as a woman, a mother, just like the patrona.

"My husband and I live comfortably, but we have made a conscious and, I believe, responsible decision to have only one child so we can provide a good lifestyle and education for him." She touched Elena's hand. "I understand accidents happen. But did you ever consider . . . other options?"

"No, señora. Never."

A few weeks later, the woman accused Elena of stealing and fired her. The missing object in question was a necklace her husband had given her for an anniversary. Elena said she hadn't seen it, but the woman insisted on searching her pockets and bag, fingering the lining as a customs officer might do. She found nothing because Elena had taken nothing. But the woman kept her last paycheck as compensation anyway.

Elena worried something might happen to her before she made it home from work each day. A police interception or an accident. Something that would separate her from her kids. If she could cut her commute and avoid buses, she would be safer. She rented an apartment above a liquor store in the town where she cleaned houses, across the hall from an Irish couple with a daughter Karina's age. She enrolled the children in school and paid the Irish woman to pick them up each afternoon and look after them until she came home.

The church down the street had a food pantry and donated a sofa bed and coats for the winter. The children weren't even baptized, but the priest didn't mind and told Elena to come back if she ever needed him. One day she went to his office in the Rectory and told him her children's father had been taken long ago and she and Karina were still vulnerable. If they came for them, she feared what would happen to Nando. She'd heard of parents deported and their citizen kids left behind, sent to foster care, trafficked, or left homeless.

The priest told Elena that whenever she felt a threat, she could come to the church for sanctuary. The deporters couldn't touch them there, and they would be safe. He gave her his private number and told her the children should memorize it. But, he warned, sanctuary was not secret. By law the church would have to inform officials they were there. It wasn't a decision to take lightly, he said, because once you enter, you can't leave until your miracle comes. It's another kind of limbo. One without daylight or fresh air.

Karina and Nando already knew to fear police. To them, regular cops and ICE were one and the same. They understood they were not as free as other people walking on the street and could be flagged for their complexions. Elena had received advice early on from the residents of the Sandy Hill house and made it the family protocol: *See a police officer on the street, find a way to dip into a store or turn onto another corner and out of sight. Police are not your friend. Even the cordial ones. Yes, they are there to help people in danger just like you're taught in school,* she'd tried to explain to her children, *but in this country some people think the ones they need protection from are us.*

SEVENTEEN

At the prison on the mountain, the staff brought in a woman who took a few girls into a room where they sat cross-legged on floor cushions. The lady was rich enough that she wore diamonds and told the girls she'd traveled to India and the Far East, studying different techniques for altering one's consciousness. A girl asked what that was supposed to mean, but the lady said never mind, she'd show them if they were willing to close their eyes and listen. She spoke in a soft voice, told the girls to picture themselves far from the prison walls, letting their imaginations take them somewhere they felt completely free. She suggested the beach, described the white foam and lapping waves, soft sand under their feet, until a girl called out that most of them had never been anywhere near an ocean.

Then the lady told the girls to pretend they were birds flying over their mountains and valleys on a day with no clouds so they could see every grassy pleat, indigo lake, and river twine. The towns below were pastel and bone-colored formations squaring churches and plazas. Cattle-freckled pastures, the plastic-sheeted nurseries where orchids and roses are grown for export; cars and buses taking people from their jobs to their families.

"A busy world, a peaceful world," the woman said. "You are a part of that world."

She instructed the girls to imagine themselves light, almost weightless, carried by their long feathers, hollow avian bones.

"Now return to your lives in the present."

She had them note the hard ground beneath their cushions, discomfort and tension in their hips and knees. The stiffness of their spines from cold seeping into the old unheated prison-school building so they existed in a permanent low-grade shiver.

"Remember where you are right now," she said, as if they could forget. "Take in your heaviness, your loneliness, how far you are from everyone who cares about you. Think about what brought you to serve your time. It is your crime and the decisions that led to it that will keep you shackled to toxic soil and prevent you from soaring as you are meant to do."

Some of the girls sighed, bored by another obvious tactic to get them to feel regret. Talia wondered why the staff cared so much about contrition when they were already being punished. She asked to use the bathroom. The meditation lady gave her a disappointed stare but nodded.

"I have to go too," said Lorena, who was there for setting her bedroom on fire after her mother wouldn't let her go to a party.

Soon everyone was saying they had to piss. A group effort to reclaim what little power they had on that mountain, or just to make their day more interesting. Later, Sister Susana called Talia to her office. She'd heard Talia initiated the bathroom revolt during the meditation workshop.

"You want me to be sorry for having to do what is only natural?"

"I've been reviewing your file. It's time for you to write a letter of apology to the man you hurt. I think it will be healing for both of you."

"I don't need to be healed, and I don't need to be forgiven."

"Write it anyway."

"He's the one who killed a defenseless animal for fun. I did what was fair."

"It's not up to you to decide who deserves retribution."

"Then why is it up to a judge and now you how to discipline me?"

Talia remembered that meeting when she trapped Sister Susana with the pillowcase the night the girls fled. The old nun who thought she knew it all.

She never wrote the letter, but Horacio's face started coming to Talia's mind more often. She'd look out the dormitory window, worrying how she was going to get out of there and make it back to Bogotá in time for her flight, and suddenly his face would obscure her vision; skin raw, eyes swollen shut, and she'd try to will him out of her head, wondering if the others were right: she was as much of a beast as he was.

The road signs for Barbosa became more frequent. Aguja pulled into a gas station and as he fueled up, they listened to a pair of viejos at another pump arguing about the peace accord recently ratified by Congress. One man in a sombrero vueltiao, face shriveled as old fruit, said the guerrillas would never abandon the monte or their criminal activity, that they were made only for battle. The other man, wishbone-legged, insisted that if only to end the massacres of the last decades, a meager treaty was better than none at all. "Talking about the past, the violence, is like digging up the dead," he said. "The pursuit of peace is the only way to give those who died a proper funeral."

Aguja returned the gas nozzle to its cradle. "You hear that, niña? You're leaving our country when things are starting to get good."

"Just because I'm leaving doesn't mean I won't come back."

"Sure you'll come back, but you'll be different."

In the gas station bathroom, she found a urine-coated floor, shit-lined toilet rim. A stench like death. At the facility, Talia was often made to clean lavatories. It was supposedly old-fashioned to assign labor as castigation, but the nuns must have been nostalgic. If a girl was caught cursing or breaking some rule, off to the toilets she was sent to scrub caked menstrual blood and stains from the graying bowls. Talia never cared though. She was used to cleaning. She'd grown up in Perla's lavandería until it went out of business and Mauro rented it to a dog groomer that went out of business too.

When her grandmother lost control of her body, forgetting how to speak, to eat, and everything else, Talia was the one who changed the liners of her underpants and washed her clothes when she soiled them. It didn't bother Talia. Her father said it was a gift to care for someone who once took care of you, and love can cure what medicine can't.

Together, they nursed Perla. Talia tried to wake her sleeping mind with the stories she'd raised her on, like the one about the boy Perla knew in childhood who ate seeds and grew watermelons in his belly that a farmer cut out of him every spring and then sewed him back up for the next harvest. Or about Eutémia, the distant cousin who brushed her hair so much that vanity turned it blue and she had to cut it all off.

Talia's favorite story was of Don Ismael, who lived on the banks of the Río Magdalena and could wave his hands in the air to make rain start or stop in order to control the river swells and floods. Talia longed for his powers, wishing he could restore her grandmother's memory, resurrect her dying body the same way he could draw water from the sky.

•   •   •

When she returned to the motorcycle, she found Aguja waiting, hands at his sides, and got the feeling this might be goodbye. He'd already taken her as far as he agreed. She pulled the French guy's wallet out of her pocket and handed it to him.

"I was thinking we could go a bit farther together," he said. "Chiquinquirá is only about fifty kilometers south. My mother will kill me if she finds out I was so close and didn't stop to light a candle in her name. You can come with me if you want. I mean, it's still on your way. From there I'm sure you can find a bus to take you to the capital."

Soon it would be dark. Night in the mountains was nothing like in the city, forever aglow with eight million lives, car beams, apartment windows, and streetlights.

"I'll go with you, but I can't pay any more than what I've already offered you."

"I know."

He mounted the motorcycle, and Talia arranged herself around him once again. When they returned to the road, silenced by the engine throb and rumble, she rested her cheek against his shoulder blade, shutting her eyes to the wind.

EIGHTEEN

Someone recommended Elena for a cleaning job in a town flanking the Hudson. It was a big house down a forested road, up a winding path behind an iron gate. Ivory-shingled with coned roofs, somehow inspired by château architecture without being completely tacky. The bosses were a married couple with generations of money behind them and a son who seemed to hate everyone except Elena. Soon the couple asked her to swap cleaning to be his nanny instead. It went so well that they asked Elena to move in and outfitted the cottage at the back of their property for her family. It was bigger and had more bedrooms than any basement or apartment she and the children had ever lived in. Residing in the bosses' town also meant a better school system for her kids.

Her charge, Lance, is now twelve. Every morning, Elena helps him get ready to take the bus to a school for children like him, and waits for him by the gate every afternoon when he gets dropped off. He doesn't speak much, but when he does there is a lot of yelling. He doesn't like to be touched by anyone, even his parents, but he will hold Elena's hand.

Karina and Nando treat him like another sibling since he doesn't have any of his own. No friends either. He likes when Nando walks with him around the yard or sits in the grass, sketchpad in hand, and shows him how to draw flowers and birds. With Karina, he likes to observe the fish and turtles in the pond, listening to her give each a name and imagine a family story in which all species are kin.

Sundays are family days, but sometimes Elena's employers call on the intercom, asking for help with their son, frustrated the books they've read and experts they've consulted provide no code with which to decipher the enigma of their son, his rages that only subside in Elena's presence. Once, Señora Tracy told Elena she wonders if the universe gave her a son like Lance because her husband was married to another woman when she met him. She asked Elena if she thought life collected debts as it went along. She thought of her son as a half-bloomed flower and tried fertility treatments for many years, like her husband wanted, as if her body were a catalog and they were placing an order for a new, improved child. Sometimes Tracy weeps for hours in her room, and other days she asks Elena to take photos of her cooking or posed on the sofa reading, and then she posts these photos on the internet for strangers to admire. Elena hears her employers tell people that Elena loves Lance as if he were her own son. It's true. She does love the boy. But her love for her own children is different, marrowed beyond bloodlines, picked from their terrain, dusted off their mountains. In their dark eyes and amber skin she sees her cloud-cast city; her ancestors, her mother, everything her family has ever been and ever will be.

Elena sent Talia back to live with Perla with the idea that she would raise the baby for a little while until Elena could send for her return. When you leave one country for another, nobody tells you years will bleed together like rain on newsprint. One year becomes five and five years become ten. Ten years become fifteen.

She never thought that when she left on the plane with Mauro it would be the last time she saw her mother in the flesh.

When Perla started forgetting her words, Mauro asked if he

could take her to a doctor. But Perla thought every ailment could be solved with polvos from a curandero or pills from a creative pharmacist. One saw a doctor only when giving birth or near death. Mauro found a doctor who agreed to come to the house. Perla protested through the examination, but when the doctor asked her to name her grandchildren, not even Talia's name came to memory. That night she collapsed as she walked from her bedroom to the bathroom. When Mauro found her on the floor of the hall, he said she looked not shaken or hurt but bewildered, and as he and Talia knelt by her side it was clear she'd forgotten where she was and who they were.

Elena felt guilty for sending Talia to be looked after by Perla. Then Talia became her grandmother's caretaker. Mauro said Talia acquired Perla's best traits, tending to her gently, washing her so she wouldn't be subject to the indignity of being bathed by Mauro. Talia dressed her. Combed her hair. Fed her, making sure Perla chewed and swallowed each bite so she wouldn't choke, because the doctor warned that she would lose the reflexes needed for eating. She was like a baby, the doctor said, and like an infant, they'd have to keep her from harming herself.

The doctor told Mauro there was no hope for improvement. She would only decline, though Mauro never shared that with Talia. He didn't want his daughter to see her grandmother's condition as a death sentence. He didn't want her to fear the body's natural process as it was shutting down, preparing for its exit from life. He wanted her to see that as long as Perla took breaths and had a heartbeat, even if her own home and family felt unfamiliar to her, she was loved and valued and still so alive, and though they could no longer reach or understand her, and her expression became a blank, secretive mask, she would know through their touch and voices that she was safe and belonged there.

Mauro told Elena the official diagnosis was progressive supra-nuclear palsy and Karina went to the library and found as much information as she could. She brought home books they spread on the kitchen table in the cottage, looking at the diagrams of halved human brains while Karina read and explained their meaning. The disease, she said, was degenerative, with no cure. A slow erasure of everything that was recognizable about Perla to them and to her.

When she said goodbye to Perla and to her country, Elena had been left with the feeling that she'd deceived her mother. The feeling grew heavier when she chose to stay in the United States with Karina and Nando after Mauro was sent home. The fissure of not being present for the end of her mother's days was one from which she knew she would not recover. She considered scenarios in which they could all be reunited. She could return to Bogotá to live in the house in Chapinero and care for her mother, but then she might never be allowed back in the United States. She would have to leave Karina and Nando behind, potentially with Toya or other friends from Sandy Hill. Or she would bring them back home with her so they could know there was a land where they truly belonged, and even if they'd never had the relationship Talia had with Perla, they would know what it was to have an abuela who loved them, and could get to know their father again too.

But then practicalities came to mind. Karina, like Elena, would have to wait years for a chance at permission to return to the only country she knew. If Nando and Talia were to return to the country of their births, they would have to leave their mother, father, and sister, and endure the same sentence of separation Elena lived. Every way she could imagine it, the family would be split. And so, Elena chose to stay.

On the computers her employers gifted each of her children, she sometimes opened the screen to a program Karina taught her to use, sliding the cursor over the earth until she found Colombia from above, narrowing in on the capital in the leathered altiplano, sweeping her finger over the roping mountains as if she were a bird coasting across the plateau, drawing in closer until she found her street, her house. She adjusted the image till it was as if she stood on the sidewalk outside the lavandería door, a dream she reenacted many times through technology, but when she showed her kids the picture of her home, they met her with puzzled expressions at how the decrepit building on the screen could be the place she so missed and loved.

Mauro said Perla died in her sleep. Elena knew it before he called. She felt an icy draft spread over her as she slept in Lance's room with him curled into her the way her own children used to do. Her heart roused. She lost her breath and knew her mother was gone.

When Mauro found Perla in the morning, she looked peaceful, as if she'd just closed her eyes seconds before. She was cold and hard to the touch, but he couldn't stop Talia from running into the room and throwing herself over her grandmother's body.

He said he could feel Elena in the room with them, as if she were in the air or in the plume of light parting the curtains. Elena told him it was true. She had been there with them. Even as she lay in that twin bed with a boy who was not her own in a house that was not her own in a country that was not her own. For those minutes, as the one who gave her life, the one she created life with, and the life she created, held one another and her mother's spirit slipped away, they were together again.

NINETEEN

You already know me. I'm the author of these pages.

There is more to the story of me, but this is what you need to know for now: I've had borders drawn around me all my life, but I refuse to live as a bordered person. I hate the term *undocumented*. It implies people like my mother and me don't exist without a paper trail. I have a drawer full of diaries and letters I never sent to my grandmother, my father, even to my younger sister that will prove to anyone that I am very real, most definitely documented; photos taped to our refrigerator, snapshots taken at the Sandy Hill house or other friends' fiestas, the Sears portraits our mother used to dress us up for every year, making us sit on bus seats still as statues so we wouldn't wrinkle to have a perfect picture to send back to her mother. Don't tell me I'm undocumented when my name is tattooed on my father's arm.

This assigned status wants you to think of the US government as another kind of parent. The one who rejects you for its preferred child. Sometimes I feel bad for having ever longed for those papers, like who I am isn't enough. Why should I want to be identified as gringa, reciting the pledge they made me memorize in school before I even understood English, if the government makes it so clear they don't want people like me here? Maybe that I don't have the documentation they want is good. It means they don't own me.

I told my brother we should make a sign to hold up at the airport when we pick up Talia that says WELCOME TO KILL YOURSELF, NEW JERSEY. Nando said she'd get on the next plane back to Colombia and our mom would die of sadness.

It was a joke, but not really. I figured Talia would eventually learn there is no place that can turn a person suicidal with the quickness of a North American suburb. Every now and then someone at school has a go. Usually a white girl, but sometimes a white boy. A few years back a teenager leaped off the Fort Lee cliffs. The town made a big production of its devastation. A lot of the girls said he was a show-off and started thinking of ways to compete with more dramatic final exits, like diving off a Manhattan skyscraper or something retro like lying across train tracks.

Every time there's a suicide attempt, the school administrators hold meetings for parents to learn how to help their miserable children, and it's expected everyone attends or your parents will be seen as uncaring assholes. Our mother went once, but when she got home she said she didn't understand how these kids who had everything they could possibly want in life—nice homes, parents who didn't abandon them, food, clothing, cars, debt-free college educations waiting to be claimed—somehow had no desire to live. She's convinced depression is a gringo problem and since Nando and I have Andean blood, we are spared.

She doesn't know that when I was a freshman who managed to get the second highest grade point average in class, I had a total fucking freak-out in the girls' bathroom, couldn't breathe, a crushing in my chest, pierced by an awareness that I was about to die, and ended up in the school shrink's office.

"You're having an anxiety attack," the lady explained. She wanted to tell my mom so she could arrange support, find me a therapist or some crap.

I said there was no money for that. She called home, but Mami was working, so she left a message saying she was concerned about my ability to cope with stress and suspected I was experiencing depressive feelings.

"¿Qué dice?" Mami asked.

"It's my English teacher. She wanted to let you know I'm the best student in her class."

She was satisfied with this, and the next time I saw the school shrink, I told her my mother said not to bother her at home anymore with stuff I can deal with myself.

There are things I wanted to tell my sister before her arrival. Like that you can love the United States of Diasporica and still be afraid of it. The day after the last election, some kids came skipping into homeroom like a war was won. Hearing cocaine jokes and mechanical hallway insults of *Go back to your country* was nothing new for me and Nando, but there was new brazenness, like a gloved hand reaching for our throats, reminding us we were not welcome.

I'm our mother's interpreter when she comes to talk to our teachers or when her bosses can't make themselves understood with their college Castellano. I can toss around phrases, carry conversations, sing along with reggaetón, but my Spanish grammar is shit and Nando and I probably have kindergarten vocabulary. We didn't speak English till we started school. They put us in the ESL program for a few years. I did all I could to get out and kill my accent, but Nando slid into the remedial trap, which is where they put the undesirables, poor kids and minorities who aren't math or science whizzes. Another word I hate: *minority*. A way to imply we're outnumbered (we're not), and suggest we are *less than*.

It's kind of amazing how rapidly language is diluted if not altogether lost, quicker than memories, which I still have of Colombia. A house of dark wooden walls, permeated with gentle voices and the tang of soap. A sky vast as an ocean. My father holding me atop a crater, silver water below. You want to say I was only a baby when I left. How could I possibly remember anything? But the pictures and scents come from a place deeper than recall. I wish I could see it again, but that's the thing about being paperless. This country locks you in until it locks you out.

I also remember the day Talia was born. We lived then in a yolk-yellow room that reeked of pizza, and this must be why I can't stand the taste of it. Our parents were gone a long time. The lady watching us couldn't pry me and Nando from the window above the alley, topped with snow. Then our parents arrived, something bundled and round in our mother's arms.

"This is your sister," she said, and Nando started crying.

Mami lowered herself to us, and I remember reaching for the baby's face. "Suave, suave," she said, as I felt the baby's fuzz of hair and warm cheeks.

At night we slept in a family tangle, my head on my father's chest, hard and flat under my small body. One day he was gone. The mattress huge and empty without him.

I've wondered if he remembers these things as often and as intensely as I do. In the years since he was taken, I've guessed at why he didn't call more. If he didn't miss us as much as we missed him. Or if it was his plan all along to deliver us to this country and leave us here alone. When we did speak on the phone, I worried he was just dealing with Nando and me like you deal with an old bill you forgot to pay or some stinky chunk of meat you've left on the kitchen counter too long.

If I were completely honest, I'd tell Talia I've always been jealous of her. She might think me nuts since, from where she stands, it might look like Nando and I got the better life deal while she was stuck with our drunk dad and dying abuela. But I sensed our mother saw Talia as her lost treasure, something she lived her whole life in hope of reclaiming, that even with two children holding on to her as we slept after our father was gone, the child our mother most loved was the one she couldn't touch because she'd sent her away.

TWENTY

You asked me to tell you what happened, and I said hell no. Then you said write it down because you're putting together a record of our family, so this is the best I can do.

We've been trying to pass since we moved to this town. You were the one who told me performing Anglo is in how you walk, talk, and dress. It's in how you think, what you spend your money on when you have it. It's in what you love and who you hate. You said if I believed I was one of them, they might believe it too.

I try to avoid them, but they always find me. Like one time on the hot-food line in the cafeteria, this kid pinched my neck from behind calling me spic boy and little Escobar, asking when I'm going to get the fuck out of the country already. I pushed my tray along the counter, hoping the lunch lady who saw and heard would say something, but she didn't.

I was talking to Emma back then. She wears one of those Irish rings with the heart pointed out and is seriously into ballet. We had our photography elective together. We were learning to use the old kind of cameras and develop prints. She hated how the chemicals burned her nostrils, so I did her darkroom work for her. We took photos of each other. Me, against the wall behind the science wing, staring at a tree branch like it was calling my name. Emma, pulling one of her legs to her ear.

When we spread our prints on the table she said my eyes are amazing, like someone just carved me open.

Like a fucking pumpkin, some dude I've never even talked to said, elbowing his way between Emma and me. Everything that followed was shit I've heard before. Even on the news. To Emma: Don't you know his people are rapists? To me: You'd better leave her alone, latrino, or I'll make a little phone call and have your whole family deported.

Latrino. That was a new one. I got a whiff of his jock funk, saw Emma's eyes lower like she was bound to him out of some secret loyalty. Next class she had a note for the teacher saying she couldn't develop prints because of her allergies, so he assigned someone else to do hers for extra credit.

The last time I went to the principal with complaints about this sort of thing, she called three of the guys who were harassing me down to her office to get their side of the story. I was hopeful because the school staff was being extra sensitive, since a few weeks before when that kid in Florida busted into his school and killed seventeen people. We sat in a row of chairs facing her desk. She asked if it was true that they called me names and threatened my family.

These guys gave looks like someone trash-talked their mothers. One said, Frankly, I'm offended Fernando would even suggest such a thing. We've only tried to befriend him since we noticed he's had a hard time fitting in at our school.

The principal turned to me. I know English is not your first language, Fernando, so it's possible you may have misunderstood what your classmates have been saying to you. As you can see, their only interest is in helping you fit in with our community.

That's when I realized rich kids make for great criminals. After school, they followed me home. Watched in a car as I waited for the bus, driving behind until I got off at the stop down the road from our house, where there are only fields and horses around. They pulled onto the grass. Two guys jumped out and yanked me into the back seat. Punched me all over. Air left my lungs. But they didn't touch my face, so when they pushed me out near our gates, though I could barely walk, Mom's first thought when she saw me dragging myself up the driveway wasn't that I'd had the shit kicked out of me but that I was coming down with the flu.

She helped me into bed and went to prepare me some caldo de pollo. I couldn't tell her the truth. You only found out because those assholes took a video of the beating and sent it to their friends. And then they sent it to you and texted if you let them give it to you up the ass they'd leave me alone. You were crying when you told me this and that there was nothing to be done. I said I could get a Taser. Electrocute their balls off next time they touched me or threatened you. You made me cross my heart that I wouldn't.

I remember wondering what it must feel like to belong to American whiteness and to know you can do whatever you want because nobody you love is deportable. Your worst crime might get you locked up forever but they'll never take away your claim to this country. We both agreed telling anyone else would only bring attention to our family. You said you hate this place, and I hugged you even though it hurt my body and we aren't really huggers anymore.

When Mom checked on us after dinner, we'd already sworn to each other not to say a word of what happened. When she asked how I was feeling, I said her soup had done its job, I was almost back to normal.

TWENTY-ONE

It should have occurred to them that by the time they'd arrive in Chiquinquirá it would be dark and cold and they'd be hungry and need a place to sleep, but it didn't. The basilica was closed for the day. Aguja would have to wait till morning to visit the Virgin. They didn't have enough money for a hotel room. It was Aguja's idea to return to the town boundary, to a pedestrian bridge suspended over a thin river. Talia followed as he lowered the motorcycle down the ridge, resting it under the bowed branches of a roble tree. He lay beside it and made a pillow of his jacket.

"We'll freeze if we sleep out here," Talia said.

"Our bodies were made for this climate. Do you think our ancestors had electric heaters?"

"They had fire."

"Keep complaining. The sun won't come up any quicker."

She sat beside him, knees pressed tight to her chest, felt the chill of the grass through her clothes.

"You can let your back touch the ground," he said. "Nothing will happen to you."

"I'm cold."

"Lay next to me. It will warm us both."

She leaned back, settling against him as their bodies aligned. "If you touch me the wrong way I'll dig out both your eyeballs."

"I don't know why you want to leave the country. You're obviously a guerrillera by nature."

It occurred to her that if he smelled this badly, she must smell bad too. Their odors comingled from being pressed together through exhaust clouds, behind trucks and buses on highways and country roads. Self-conscious, she tried to tilt herself away, but he pulled her in closer. She felt his bones against her shoulder. He adjusted his arm to cradle her neck and set his palm against her side.

"Are you going to tell me the truth of how you ended up so far from home?"

"I told you. I was trying to get away from a bad guy."

"But what were you doing in Barichara of all places?"

It had been only days since she'd fled from the prison school, but Talia felt she'd been lying for a very long time, maybe her whole life. She decided to give him as much honesty as she thought he could handle without being tempted to turn on her.

"I ran away."

"From where?"

"A place they sent me for not being good."

He laughed. "I believe that."

"You wouldn't make a joke if you knew what I did to be sent there."

"Did you slap some other girl at school?"

"I hurt a man badly. I burned him and scarred him for life."

"How?"

"With hot oil."

He was quiet. She heard the chime of the river current. Above, starlight refracted, the moon cloud-narrowed to a bullet.

"Does your mother know what you've done?"

"No."

"So you're a fugitive."

"I suppose."

"You know what happens to fugitives when they flee the country? You can never come back. If you do, the police will be waiting to send you to prison."

"I'm not some drug trafficker or politician. I'm only fifteen."

She felt his fingers light on her hair but didn't tell him to stop.

"Are you ready to leave this country knowing you might never be able to return?"

"I don't want to think about that."

"When you get to the United States, nobody will understand you. I don't mean just the language. It's a country of strangers. It will be another kind of sentence. But one that as an immigrant you won't be able to escape."

"You think this country is so much better?"

"No, but it's a land of brothers and sisters. You want to go to a place where you'll be invisible."

"I want to be with my mother."

"Colombia is your mother too."

Aguja slept, but Talia remained awake on the bed of hard earth, deafened by the river. At home, when she couldn't sleep, she'd go to her father's room and ask him to tell her the story of how Chiminigagua created the sun, named Sué, and then his wife, Chía, the moon. Though they were loving companions, they argued over who should control the world through day and night. Since Chía watched the world through the darkness, Mauro said Talia should ask her help to guide her into a peaceful sleep until her husband, Sué, took over the care of the world at daybreak.

Usually Talia fell asleep still whispering her petition to the moon, and when she awoke to the apartment bathed in morning light, her father, with breakfast ready in the kitchen, told his daughter she must be special because the moon always listened to her.

She knew she would never know another night like this one. Not beside Aguja and not under flaring stars like nails hammered into the sky, the waft of dirt and mint and flowers, the murmur of the arroyo flowing toward the Río Magdalena to the mouth of the Caribbean Sea, where sharks fed on the burst of river fish. *This land, with all its beauty, still manages to betray itself,* she remembered her father saying. If this were true, and she was one if its children, it was no mystery why she turned her back on it just as her parents had done before her.

She thought of what would be gained and what would be lost once she left.

In the other country, she would embrace her mother and siblings for the first time since she was a baby. They would all sleep under the same roof.

In the other country, she would fall in love for the first time. The thought thrilled her. But then she thought in this country she may never find love and felt blighted.

In the other country, an uncharted future awaited. But it could only be so if she let her future in this country die.

In the other country, she would no longer be a criminal. But in the other country half her family was and always would be.

In the other country, she would have a sister and a brother. No longer a lone child caring for her grandmother's health and her father's heart.

In the other country, there would be no boy like Aguja sleeping beside her, who felt familiar the first time she saw his face, who knew hers too.

He was right. In the other country there would only be strangers and she would be a stranger, too, even to her own family. Her father would wait in Colombia, perhaps forever, for a daughter and a family who had learned to live without him.

What would have happened if she'd not gone to meet Claudia at the restaurant by El Campín that day, if there had been no kitten, if she hadn't been in the alley when the cooks took their break, or if the man had shown mercy or indifference, left the creature alone rather than make the decision to kill, and if Talia, instead of reacting in fury had hung back in horror? His small yet barbaric act had showed Talia her own darkness, and she would never be the same. What if she'd never escaped her prison school and instead completed her sentence of just a few more months? At eighteen, after demonstrating reformation, they said her crime would be erased from her record. It would be something she could forget if she tried. But Talia was impatient as thunder. She wanted to believe her mother's love unconditional but was afraid if Elena discovered what she'd done, what she was capable of and where her crime took her, she'd change her mind about having her long-distance child live with her. Sometimes Talia was grateful Perla died when she did. If she'd lived to see her beloved granddaughter sent to prison, it would have killed her.

Talia stood up and went to the stream, shallow and clear unlike the curdled arteries of the Río Bogotá. She squatted by the downed reeds, running her fingers through the waterline, skimming pebbles settled into the embankment. Her father once told her that river stones are good luck for journeys because waterways are peopled with spirits traveling between worlds, grazing those stones, leaving them as talismans for the living.

TWENTY-TWO

A flock of buses brought pilgrims to the basilica the next morning. Talia and Aguja watched the crowd thicken. He asked Talia one last time if she was sure she didn't want to come instead of waiting on a bench. She was sure, she said, and watched him make his way to join the faithful. Perla had never been to the basilica but always lit candles and went to Mass on the Virgin's feast days. She kept a statue of the blue-caped Santa María in her white veil on a table next to her bed. When she was small, Talia pretended it was a statue of Elena and her even if the baby in her ceramic arms was a boy. After Perla died, when Mauro sold the house and they prepared to move into an apartment, he packed the statue in newspaper, but the movers lost it and they never saw it again. Talia cried because she felt the statue, despite the Virgin's chipped hand and missing nose, carried a piece of her grandmother, and without the house or the dust of her remains, which they'd sent to Elena, there was nothing of Perla left.

It was as if she'd never existed. As if Talia had imagined her entire childhood in her abuela's care. No proof of her voice, and now Talia could only hear it in memory. They'd given away her clothes and even the repaired crucifix in the foyer she'd loved as if it were another husband was donated to a church near Paloquemao. When Talia left, she would be able to take even less with her. Just a suitcase of clothes and a few things to remind her of home. Her father said the death of a loved one was like a house on fire. Even with everything intact, it still felt like mere ashes.

Soon he'd be left in their small apartment without Talia sleeping in the next room. She wondered if for him his daughter's absence would be another house on fire.

When he returned from the basilica, Aguja handed Talia a paper pouch. She opened it and pulled out a mess of string attached to a plastic scapular with the face of the Virgin on it.

"For protection." He pulled down the collar of his shirt to show an identical string around his neck. "I lit a candle for you too. So you'll make it back to your mother with no problems."

She thanked him and slipped the scapular over her head, felt it dangle against her chest.

"I should get back to Barichara. My girlfriend must be having a heart attack. I haven't even called her. What's your plan for the rest of the way?"

"I'm going to try to get on one of those buses."

"They're charters. They'll never let you on. It's only two or three hours' drive from here to the city. Why don't you just ask your father to pick you up?"

"He doesn't have a car."

"You don't have any other friend to do you the favor?"

"I'm afraid anyone I call would turn me in."

After a moment he said, "I guess I could take you. I'll feel better if I know you made it back safe. I don't want to wonder about you, you know?"

"Your girlfriend is going to think you got kidnapped."

"I kind of did."

Before leaving Chiquinquirá for the capital, Aguja called home. He stepped away for privacy, but Talia could hear him tell his girl he got caught up visiting a friend in another town and would be back soon, assuring her, no, he wasn't with another girl, that she was the only one for him and didn't he prove it every day when he asked her to marry him and she was the one who insisted they were still too young and should wait? He told her he loved her. Called her sweet names. Preciosa, muñequita, mi angelito de la guarda. His voice was liquid, a different register from the one he used with Talia. Even his posture changed, holding the phone against his cheek as if it were his girl's hand. Talia tried to picture her, considering how some girls became special to boys while others were forgettable.

Before they went on their way again, Talia asked if she could use his phone. She thought it was time to call her father, let him know she'd made it this far and that she'd be home in a matter of hours. Aguja's phone was down to its last drops of charge, but he handed it over. She dialed and let it ring and ring, but there was no answer.

TWENTY-THREE

Mauro saw a missed call on his phone from a number he didn't recognize. No message was left. He hoped it was Talia calling to say she was safe, then panicked that it was the police or a hospital reporting that she'd been arrested or hurt. He was at one of the apartments at his job, fixing a light fixture for some residents. As he worked on wires, he took in the sight of the family seated at their dining room table eating breakfast. The parents, a son, two daughters. Just like his family except not like them at all, so comfortable in their routine they mostly ignored one another. The father read the morning paper. The mother gave instructions to the housekeeper as she refreshed their coffees. The children mute with boredom. Mauro could not fathom the luxury of such familial indifference.

The father, wearing a pressed shirt and trousers, a suit jacket slung over the back of another chair, started talking about the peace treaty, calling it a farce, speculating which side would be the first to cheat the other. One of the daughters said the rebel forces had already demobilized and surrendered their arms, and the father said they weren't fools enough to give up every weapon in their arsenal; they surely had hidden stockpiles. He predicted the official peace would bring dissension from revolutionary fringes, smaller factions would gain power, and insurgents already legitimized by the treaty would turn Colombia into a formalized guerrilla nation.

He spoke loudly in a way typical of the Latin American man of a certain class, presumed authority, each an aspiring president of their own miniature republic. The father told his children they were too young to remember the massacres of the Awá in Nariño or the mass killings in Dabeiba and Chocó; an era when more parents buried their children than the other way around. Everybody wanted a peace parade, a Nobel Prize, and a new national holiday so badly they'd forgotten the hundreds of thousands dead and still missing.

As Mauro worked to restore light to the family's hallway, he felt imperceptible. The kids had passed him in the lobby many times. They'd been raised to know some people merit polite greetings and others can go without. The father asked his name after Mauro helped him jump-start his car one day. After that, whenever he saw Mauro he would say, "How's the family, Mauricio?" even though Mauro never told him anything about Elena or his children. The wife had visits from women friends most afternoons. Once, he was called when the kitchen sink flooded during a gathering. The wife was frantic as the housekeeper mopped the froth. A few days later the wife found Mauro in the lobby and asked if he knew anyone she could hire because her current housekeeper was leaving.

Mauro closed his eyes for a few seconds to try to trick himself, then opened them. For one suspended moment, he succeeded. There was his own family seated at the table: Mauro and Elena, each distracted by the details of the day, a life where ominous news headlines only infiltrated their nonviolent world as mealtime conversation. The children. His son, angular and slouched, an expression still hopeful, unmarked by the rejection Mauro had known as a boy, and not a hint of the desertion Mauro had imposed on his own kids. His first daughter. A face like her mother's, serene but withholding.

Talia was there, too, the one he worried had been so protected she'd become too fearless. He blinked again and they disappeared.

With the lavandería closed and no more prospective tenants for the shop below, the upkeep of Perla's house became too expensive for Mauro to afford, even with Elena's contributions from abroad. Mauro suggested renting out rooms, but Elena didn't want her childhood home converted into a hostel or boardinghouse. The surrounding blocks were filling with cafés, galleries, bars, and trendy shops, though theirs was still untouched. Compared to the newer buildings coming up in the area, Perla's house only looked more decayed. Every potential tenant remarked the same thing. The structure would need a complete remodel. It might be worth more torn down.

"Just sell it," Elena said. She'd sign whatever papers were needed to give him the authority to do so on her behalf.

He wondered if time bleached her memories of the house so they were mere scratches on a pale canvas. No longer an inheritance but a gorge of debt, a place she didn't expect ever to return to much less to live. But Mauro feared losing the house would make the family even more rootless; without it and with her mother already gone, once Talia joined Elena in the United States, there would be nothing left for her in Colombia.

Before turning the keys over to the new owners, Spaniards who planned to convert the building into a language school, Mauro and Talia went to the roof, the first place he'd kissed her mother, and sat on the ledge facing the crown of Monserrate. Lightning scissored in the distance. Talia said the city was so ugly and the weather so bad, she didn't understand why the capital hadn't been founded in a better climate. Mauro reminded her it was the land of their ancestors and their connection to it ran deeper than Bogotá being designated the nation's principal city. In the time before colonization and extermination, before their language was outlawed and they were given a new god and new names, they were a potent and powerful civilization of millions.

He wanted to convey to his daughter the price of leaving, though he had difficulty finding the words. What he wanted to say was that something is always lost; even when we are the ones migrating, we end up being occupied. But Talia wasn't listening, already tiring of her father's stories. He felt her detaching from him, from their city. She saw their new apartment as a temporary place, counting down until she could leave it. What she didn't know, Mauro thought, was that after the enchantment of life in a new country dwindles, a particular pain awaits. Emigration was a peeling away of the skin. An undoing. You wake each morning and forget where you are, who you are, and when the world outside shows you your reflection, it's ugly and distorted; you've become a scorned, unwanted creature.

He knew Talia believed her journey to be a renewal, and it would be. He hoped the love of her mother and siblings would be enough to soothe her when she met the other side of the experience, when she would learn what everyone who crosses over learns: Leaving is a kind of death. You may find yourself with much less than you had before.

It seemed to Mauro that in choosing to emigrate, we are the ones trafficking ourselves. Perhaps it was the fate of man to remain in motion and seek distance, determined by the will of Chiminigagua, because humankind's first migration was from the subterranean world beneath the sacred lake, driven out by the great water snake, to the land of the jaguars and the kingdom of the condors above.

•   •   •

Elena called to ask Mauro to pack Perla's statue of the Virgen de Chiquinquirá for Talia to take on her trip north. He said it was lost in the move. They'd looked everywhere for it. He was very sorry he hadn't told her before. He worried that to Elena it was just another Mauro apology. He wanted to say he regretted not only losing the statue but all the ways he'd disappointed her, and because he hadn't yet found a way to restore their family to what they once were. But after a pause Elena only asked about Talia, why she wouldn't return her mother's calls. Mauro was relieved to change the subject but not that he'd have to lie again.

"She's just busy getting ready to leave. She can barely sleep from excitement to see you. After Saturday, you two will have all the time in the world to catch up." He wasn't sure she believed him. In fact, he was fairly certain she did not. But she didn't insist or probe anymore.

That afternoon, at a religious store on Calle 64, Mauro bought Elena a new statue, shorter and not as detailed as the one Perla had so loved, but he took it to a nearby church and asked the priest to bless it. He hoped Talia would tell Elena this much when she delivered it to her.

Mauro studied the map of Santander trying to imagine routes Talia might have taken to get home. What were the odds that a fifteen-year-old runaway girl could cross several provinces and navigate the mountains alone and unharmed? He refused to picture her hitchhiking, rain-soaked and hungry, tried not to think of where she'd been sleeping. He wondered if she'd paired up with one of the other girls as travel companions and prayed she was safe, reciting mantras that she'd soon be home, trying to conjure such a reality by preparing her luggage for her departure, her paper ticket tucked safely in a dresser drawer. Clothes folded and arranged in neat piles, packed in a suitcase he bought at El Centro Andino, its shell pink as a passiflora, her favorite flower.

He'd bought gifts for Karina and Nando. Candies, discs of Colombian music. A necklace for Karina and a leather belt for Nando. Not much but it was what he could afford, even if he was sure they were used to nicer, less folkloric things in the north. He'd taken Perla's photos out of their frames and packed them in an envelope along with a letter for Elena. He was embarrassed of his handwriting, how he hadn't stayed long enough in school for it to be shaped into something more presentable, ruining many sheets of paper trying to keep his sentences in straight lines, wanting to communicate that she was still his only love and asking her forgiveness for every way he'd fallen short.

When she returned, Talia would see her father had a gift for her too. During the years when they were getting to know each other as father and daughter, when she was still in only Perla's care, she glimpsed the ink on his forearm. She asked Mauro what it said because she couldn't yet read.

"Karina."

"Like my sister?"

He told her yes and watched her curiosity melt to hurt. Talia didn't say so, but he knew she must have wondered why Karina's was the only name written on his body. He could not explain there was no money to spend on tattoos. Karina's name had been a whim, in the euphoria of the days after her birth, when he ran to the tattoo shop that had existed then around the corner and had his arm branded with his daughter's and mother's name. He remembered when he came home to show Elena. Skin tender and bloody, covered in ointment and a clear film. She brought his arm to her lips and kissed their baby's name. The following year, when the three of them were in the United States, she would trace those same lines with her finger as if they held a kind of promise.

Now when Talia looked at her father's arms, above the calloused hands she'd rub with her perfumed lotions every night when he came home from work as had been their ritual for years, she would see her brother's name etched above her sister's, and above Nando's name, Talia's own name in filigree script.

On his other arm, otherwise unmarked except for scars from his years working in the campo and those that followed in Ciudad Bolívar and Paloquemao and the United States, on the papery flesh over the veins of his wrist, was the name he should have imprinted himself with long ago. Elena. Though he would ask Talia not to tell her mother about it. He hoped one day to be able to show her himself.

Talia was not a sentimental girl. Not like Mauro, who the world might still consider young and vibrant but to his daughter was a melancholy old man. She might think his gestures soppy and insignificant rather than seeing, as he did, that once she got on that plane, he'd have little more than his family's names carved into his arms.

The apartment, though small, would be too big for only him. The sight of his daughter's empty room, those posters of gringo singers and bands she taped to the walls, would sting. He would return to his silence, something he'd gotten a dose of during her confinement, and the thought of the unending solitude that awaited him with her returned to North America was more than he would be able to bear. Some nights he even longed for the chaos he knew when he slept on the streets because, Mauro realized, it was a distraction from the echoes of his interior. He went to his meetings nearly every evening and hoped they would be enough to keep him from his former vices during the wilderness of time he'd be sentenced to after Talia's departure.

TWENTY-FOUR

It was my idea to go to the Palisades like when we were kids, Sundays when almost everyone in the Sandy Hill house had the day off and we'd caravan north for a picnic on Hook Mountain. I'm the only one with a driver's license in our house, and Mom's bosses are cool about letting me take out their Jeep since they hardly use it and—you don't know this—I go up there on my own sometimes just to draw the view, those swirly candy colors, especially the hour before the sun slides out of sight. That day you and I walked our favorite trail up to the rocky shelf on the mountainside, took in the drop into the bruised Hudson. It looked and felt like it did when I was a kid, like the end of the earth and the end of time.

People die on that mountain. Mostly hikers who wander off the marked paths and slip from the precipice. People fall while photographing the highlands and waterway. Dogs air-bound for a Frisbee. We sat facing Sing Sing across the river. As kids we thought it was a castle where the King of America lived until someone told us it was a prison where they locked up murderers and lunatics. It was years before I understood that our father's detainment and deportation, which I don't remember at all, meant he'd spent time in jail. Maybe one like Sing Sing, with its spindly watchtowers and wire scaffolds.

Our mom tells me stories about how much he loved me. First

son, only boy, how it's supposed to be special for a man and how, before I was born, he told her about the ancient ruler of his mother's hometown whose virgin daughter became pregnant by the sun and she gave birth to an emerald that she guarded until it grew into a man who became this warrior king named Goranchacha, son of the sun. But when I see our dad through video calls, I can't help thinking of him like some distant relative. Somebody I know I'm supposed to care about even if it feels like an act. I know it's different for you, Karina. You've perfected your I-don't-give-a-fuck look, but then you hang up from one of those calls with our father and rush to your room, and I hear you pillow-cry through the walls. Then you go quiet, and I know you're writing.

That's what you do when you're not at the library or reading the books you bring home. And you write in English even though Mom acts like it's kind of a tragedy you can't write in Spanish, but I know you'd rather not worry about her reading what you write and you probably think I don't care enough to snoop. That one time I asked what was in your notebooks, you told me the government says you don't have the right papers so you're writing your own. And when things finally get fair and safe enough for people like you to come to the light, they'll have to listen to everything you've been waiting to say.

I've only ever seen our mother on her own. I know there was a time when it was different, but I can't remember our parents to-gether. Don't know their faces in love. I didn't witness them as a couple long enough to see them fight or start to hate each other like everyone else's parents till they decide they'd rather love other people instead.

What were they like? Was it one of those couplings by circum-stance, the fact of her pregnancy, or were they seriously knocked out the way everyone wants to be in love, the way you can only be when you're young and just hope it lasts and doesn't leak out of your hands or accidentally die by your touch like a newborn bird.

I only know our parents' faces as they talk to each other through digital screens. Their weird politeness, like they're business associates and didn't once fuck enough to make three babies together. It's always the same. Mom ends those calls looking disoriented and a little pained. Tell your father you love him, she mouths to us before we hang up. We love you, we say in English. Los adoro, he answers back.

I remember the time you asked our mom why she's never had a boyfriend since our dad left our family in this country. Why do you even bother being faithful, you said, I guarantee he's not living like some monk in Colombia.

It was clear your words burned. I thought she was going to tell you to stop talking like some rude gringa, one of those sitcom brats in dire need of a chancletazo, but she only sighed and said, You don't know what you're talking about, corazón.

I hope when Talia arrives she'll tell us about our father. Our mom's stories are limited to fifteen years ago and the bits she caught from her mother before she died about his life in Bogotá, and then what he reveals over the phone, which isn't much. You say your single wish is to be able to vote in this country and made me swear to register as soon as I turn eighteen so I can cast ballots in every election since you and Mom can't. But I know your even bigger wish is to have our dad in front of us, included in all our corny family photos. Learning his habits as well as we know our mother's. How she stirs her coffee with her finger instead of a spoon so she can tell how hot the water is before it touches her tongue, she says, how the sight of rain makes her release a long, whistly breath, or how on chilly days she'll always say it feels just like Bogotá. I guess what I'm trying to say is that having Talia return to us feels like a piece of our father is coming too.

• • •

You pointed across the river in the direction of Sleepy Hollow. You were talking about ghosts haunting that land, souls at unrest beneath the water, the dead buried in the mountain, sacrificed to history. I hadn't heard you talk so much in a while, so I let you go on uninterrupted. In a couple of weeks, you'd graduate high school. Second in your class, though everyone knows you tied for first but the administrators had to decide which girl got to make the big speech at graduation and they picked the other one. You told Mom that in our town, with taxes so high the school may as well be prep, they couldn't have a valedictorian who's only planning to take a class or two at the local junior college when that other girl is on her way to the Ivy League. All year long there was talk of admissions tests, college tours. Seniors chose their schools by sports teams, family legacies, weather and lifestyle. Not you. You don't get to be a part of that.

You earn your money babysitting and dog walking since none of the shops in town will hire you. You were too scared to apply for DACA when you were eligible. You said it was another trick to sniff you out in exchange for a work permit and two years of a semidocumented existence. And maybe you were right, now that the government froze the program, knows where everyone is, and can do whatever they want with that information. I know you've been thinking of ways to bring in more cash to pay for your classes since Mom forbids you to work off the books for a restaurant. But I didn't expect to see your computer left open to a site with ads looking for webcam girls. *No experience necessary. Must feel comfortable showing face and total nudity for paid subscribers. Work in studio or in comfort of your own home.* After dinner, when our mom went back to the main house to put Lance to bed, I asked what you were looking up such crazy shit for.

It's just research. I want to know what job opportunities are out there for someone like me, you said, like it was the most normal thing. Like I caught you bookmarking scholarships or financial aid funds instead.

I wanted to come down on you like you came down on me last summer when I started talking to those recruiters prowling the mall about joining the military, when you said our mom would fall into a grief coma because she didn't bring me into this world to kill or be killed, that they would use me as a bait dog and I was totally fucking expendable. The government knew it, you all knew it, the only one who didn't know it was me. You're a talented artist, you said. You need to go to art school, use what you have and become excellent, not waste your gift on learning to murder instead. I wasn't sure I believed you. I still don't know if I do. But I didn't argue, because you're the one who made the library your second home, who says if you can't go to college you can read every book there, memorize this country's narratives and myths, study history even the most educated people never learned or have forgotten, about laws written and unwritten and rewritten for people who come here looking for a better life than the one they left and people who were brought as babies, so nobody can say you're ignorant about your status, no matter how arbitrary it is, this undocumented condition they talk about like it's some disease.

All these years we've been watching out for the government and you're ready to hand yourself right over, you told me. I let you think you won the argument, but the truth is I didn't really want to go anywhere. I wanted to be convinced to stay.

TWENTY-FIVE

At the Palisades with my brother, I noticed crows swarming the river basin. I read somewhere that crows aren't usually found in estuaries and are more inland prone. People marvel at the miracle of animal instincts for migration to ensure their survival. Hippos, zebras, and lions were imported to Colombia by drug lords for private menageries, then abandoned when the arrests and extraditions began. Some animals starved, others were given refuge, and still others found ways to roam free and populate hills and valleys with their offspring. They've adapted and thrive in terrain for which they have no genetic memory. Unless you believe, as our father told our mother long ago, that the first beings traveled every inch of this earth, claiming it as home for all creatures.

Our mother was captivated lately by the news story of a Colombian woman lost in the Amazon jungle for nearly forty days with her three children. The fruits they found had already been eaten by animals, so they dug for seeds and worms. By day, monkeys threw their shit at them. At night they covered in sticks and leaves, though rain still drenched them, sometimes flooding to their necks, and insects burrowed in their ears, noses, and eyes. The woman held her children close while creatures approached—owls, armadillos, snakes, maybe tapirs or animals whose names she didn't even know.

In the black jungle night, she couldn't be sure. Once she heard an undeniable jaguar call and knew it could be their end. She prayed it wouldn't track their scent and never heard it again. She believed the forest duende, said to be fond of mestizo children, made them get so lost they couldn't find their own footprints and protected them now, though not from the ticks and maggots fattening on their blood that they pulled from their raw feet and open wounds. She told her story from a hospital in Putumayo, where she and her children were treated for hunger, dehydration, and parasites after an Indigenous fisherman saw them drinking water from a riverbank, thin as spirits, almost too weak to stand, as if the gentlest wave might sweep them away. Our mother seemed most affected that this woman had no idea hundreds of volunteers, police, and army helicopters upturned the jungle looking for them with no luck, that she and her children had traveled so far searching for a way out that they'd left the Colombian Amazonas and entered territory claimed by Peru, and once rescued, her husband confessed that with his family lost to the selva he'd already planned his suicide.

For months now, we've also seen news stories of other divided families, children separated from their parents at the southern border. I haven't told anyone I dream of these children in particular, hear their cries, the eventual silence of capitulation, feel their ache of lost faith and unknowing. In my sleep, I am one of them. Our family didn't cross any desert or river to get here. We came by plane with the right documents, now worthless. My life, like my sister's and my brother's, is a mishap, a side effect of our parents' botched geographical experiment. I often wonder if we are living the wrong life in the wrong country. If the reason I have felt so out of place is because I, like the narco animals, have no biological or ancestral memory of this strange North American landscape or its furious seasons. These mountains and rivers are not mine. I haven't yet figured out if by the place of my birth I was betrayed or I am the betrayer, or why this particular nation and not some other should be our family pendulum.

I looked over the bluff at the tidal ponds below and thought of lives lost to the crags and current. I clawed the rock I was sitting on, closed my eyes, felt wind scarf my neck, and imagined the feeling of hurling myself over.

"What do you think it will be like when she gets here?" my brother asked.

"We'll have to look after her. Explain things. It might take a while for us to get used to each other."

"What do you think will happen to us?"

"With Talia?"

"With everything."

When he turns twenty-one, my brother can request to have our mother's status adjusted. In applying, he will have to tell them where we are. The stakes are brutal. They could deny the request and instead come for her and for me. I wasn't sure if this is what he meant with his question, so I said what I always say about our future.

"I don't know."

Then I asked myself more questions without answers: If I vaulted off this mountain what would the headline say? *An undocumented girl fell to her death.* Would they print my name, describe my life as a loss or as a waste? If the fall didn't kill me, would anyone care to record the story of my survival? I pictured being saved by some gravitational reversal, sprouting wings that would carry me from this place until I found myself among other migratory beings, bound for somewhere that feels more like home.

TWENTY-SIX

As a child, Elena's mother told her about the condor that lived deep in the cordillera, so lonely that he flew down to the valley in search of a wife. He found a girl tending to goats in her garden and asked if she would be his wife. The girl said she loved her home too much, she never wanted to leave it, and for this reason she knew she would never marry, but she didn't mind because she couldn't stand the thought of leaving her parents behind. The condor said he understood because he'd once had parents he loved until they left him alone in their nest and flew away. The next day, the condor returned and again asked the girl to be his wife. Again, she refused. This time the condor said he would leave but asked the girl if she would please first scratch a painful itch for him. He lowered himself so the girl could reach his shoulders to scratch beneath his feathers, but as she did so, he took flight with the girl still holding his back and flew to his cave in the mountains. Once there, he pulled out some of his own feathers, decorating the girl to make her his bride. At home, the girl's parents cried with worry over their missing child. A green parrot that lived nearby heard their wails, approached, and told them: "If I am able to bring your daughter home, do you promise you will always let me eat fruit from your trees and take shelter in your garden?" The parents agreed, so the parrot left to search for the girl. He found her atop a sharp peak living with the condor. By now, she'd grown her own feathers and birthed half-avian chicks that died. She was no longer human but something else. As the condor slept, the parrot took the girl back to her family. Upon her return, her feathers fell out and soon she was the girl she'd once been, happy and at peace in her home. The condor was furious and came looking for her. But the parrot was waiting in the garden where he'd been permitted to live, and when the condor tried to eat him, the parrot gathered all his might and pushed straight through the other end of the condor's body. The condor tried to eat the parrot again and again, but the parrot escaped each time out the other end, until the condor decided to tear the parrot apart with the force of its beak and crescent talons, swallowing the meaty bits, but each morsel swept through the condor's body, emerging in the form of smaller, brightly colored birds. And this was how the land came to be populated by parrots from the scarlet macaws to the tiny golden parakeets people like to keep in cages in their homes.

When they lived together in Perla's house, Mauro sometimes crept out of bed, careful not to wake Elena, and went to the roof to smoke cigarettes. He thought she never noticed, but Elena always woke to the void he left in their bed. When she followed, she'd find him staring past the veined mountain lights. Sometimes she watched and let him think he was still alone. When she did say his name, he met her with an indecipherable expression.

One night when Mauro left the bed, Karina sleeping in a crib at its foot, Elena lay still in the room thinking of her own father, a man she never knew beyond photographs Perla removed from their frames and placed in a chest that was never to be opened. In the same chest, she kept the deed to the house, bank papers, and a letter from a woman who claimed to be her husband's new wife. Elena discovered it in a closet one day, though she never told her mother. When she had her own children, Elena understood a mother is entitled to her secrets.

She heard Mauro's footsteps flat and rushed. Not his usual nocturnal choreography to avoid waking her and the baby. He came to her side and found her already awake. "Elena, I saw it. With these eyes. I saw it!"

"Saw what?" She expected he'd witnessed a car wreck or robbery on the street below. It wouldn't be the first time. Or even that he'd spotted a UFO, since the news had reported more sightings of orbs like fireballs above the Nazca lines.

"A condor flying over our barrio, and when it came to our house the wind held it above me and—" He lost his breath, dropping his face in his palms. When he pulled them away, Elena saw his eyes glossed with tears and asked him to show her.

They ran together to the roof, but there was no great bird. Not even stars. Only clouds blotting the sky.

"There are no condors in the city, Mauro."

"I saw one. I need you to believe me."

She wanted to offer some logic to make the apparition more plausible, said it might have escaped from the zoo or been blown off course from the páramo of Chingaza. Mauro had spoken before about condors. He once told Elena he'd gone with a friend up to Ciudad Bolívar and saw boys shooting a condor as it glided over the escarpment but the bird had escaped their bullets. Elena didn't believe his story, even if as a child she'd pretended Bogotá was not a city but a jungle thick as the manigua of Caquetá, the brick skins of buildings were tree bark, and police sirens were the calls of monkeys and birds.

In school, she'd learned condors preferred open tundra where they could feed easily and soar for miles without a flap of their wings. They were scarce because, besides being the national symbol of freedom and sovereignty and the largest flying creature on earth, they were believed sacred and immortal, guardians of the upper world. Their population diminished by poisonings and hunters after their bones, feathers, and organs, which were said to have healing properties.

That night, reading Elena's skepticism, Mauro asked why it was so hard to believe the condor could have returned to the city. "This was its territory before man occupied it, after all. Maybe it came to remind us what we've stolen."

Years later, when Mauro was down to his final days before deportation, he called Elena from the detention center and asked if she remembered the night he saw the condor fly over him on their roof. She told him she did.

"Do you know that when a condor is old or sick, or if its mate dies, it will push itself to fly higher than ever before, then drop out of the sky to end its own life?"

"I didn't know that."

She remembered that when they returned to their bedroom after searching for signs of the condor, they'd stood by Karina's crib, watching as she slept. Her parents' absence hadn't pulled her awake. Mauro whispered then that a condor, which could live as long as a human, was faithful to one partner for life. Together they nested on impenetrable cliffs, sharing the duties of incubation, making a home for their family only they were able to reach.

Friends told Elena that when a child and a parent are reunited after so many years apart, the distance and time can be more difficult to breech than either anticipated. They warned her not to have unrealistic expectations for her daughter's attachment to her or for her family's bonding once she arrived. She tried to prepare herself for possible outcomes. She knew that when Talia landed she might feel so overwhelmed with the deluge of English, the vacillating weather, so far from her city and mountains she might eventually beg for a return ticket home, so Elena budgeted some money in case. She would not deny her daughter the right to go back to Colombia the way she'd denied it to herself. She knew Mauro's arms would be hard for her daughter to leave and accepted that after so many years apart she likely loved her father far more.

She blamed herself for displacing her own children, especially her girls. Karina and Talia, binational, each born in one country and raised in another like repotted flowers, creatures forced to live in the wrong habitat. She'd watched the child who came to her that winter in Delaware grow through photographs and phone lines. Her voice was always new when they spoke. Her other children had lost much of their Spanish and sometimes Elena imagined it was Talia, the daughter she did not raise yet who had grown up in the same home as her mother, who knew her best.

When Karina and Nando were small, living in those cramped basements, they asked Elena why they didn't have a house of their own like the families on TV. "We have a house," she told them. "We just don't live in it because it's far away."

"But why?" they asked over and over.

"Because we live here," she would say, wishing there was a way they could comprehend what even she couldn't. She was never sure if she'd made the right decision in staying. Eventually she'd understand that in matters of migration, even accidental, no option is more moral than another. There is only the path you make. Any other would be just as wrong or right.

Lately when they spoke on the phone, Mauro told Elena the news abroad showed a United States scorching with civilian massacres as bad or worse than Colombia's ghastliest days of warfare, where ordinary American citizens were more heavily armed than any guerrilla or paramilitary fighter ever was. And was it true—he asked—the stories of cities contaminated by the water supply, children killed by police with impunity, communities left to fend for themselves against natural disasters as bad as the earthquakes and mudslides their land endured? How could people still think of gringolandia as some promised land knowing those things happened there?

She rarely remembered any danger when she thought of her homeland. Lies often accompany longing. But it was worth something that she'd never been hurt or had to hide from anyone the way she'd had to do in the United States. Her birthplace had its own bigotry, inequality, terrorism, oil spills, water contaminations, and poverty just like in the north. But every nation in the Americas had a hidden history of internal violence. It just wore different masks, carried different weapons, and justified itself with different stories. She couldn't guarantee to Mauro or to anyone that this country was safer than any other, or even that it offered more advantages or opportunity. Not anymore. She could only meet Talia with the love she'd been guarding for fifteen years. Her daughter had two countries to call home. Where she made hers would be her choice. If she ever decided to leave, Elena made a silent promise to let her daughter go.

She'd sustained herself on reverie of her family reunited in the north. Now that her youngest was due to arrive in a few days, a new dream took shape: that of returning with her children to Colombia, possibly on the day they'd spent years wishing for, when they were each granted permission to travel freely, to navigate the routes between their nations without fear of detention or exile. There, she saw Mauro waiting for them at the airport, ready to fold them into his wings.

TWENTY-SEVEN

Across the sabana, Talia's city came into view. The unexpected harmony of russet buildings, avenues the color of shrapnel shining with recent rain. She guided Aguja from her place behind him, lips close to his ear. They passed the old house, barricaded and papered with construction permits. An announcement of imminent demolition. She led him to her and Mauro's current address, the third-floor apartment opposite the widow who shared her stews with neighbors. Aguja parked his motorcycle along the sidewalk. Talia had no key, so she rang the building bell, but there was no response. She could only wait until her father came home from work and hope that in the meantime nobody recognized her.

They went to a park a few corners away. An elderly couple on a nearby bench fed crumbs to pigeons at their feet. Across the plaza, a young woman strollered a child. Talia didn't know any of these people but somehow felt acutely connected, tethered to the wooden bench, the concrete beneath her feet. A sense of her life's incompletion had led her this far, but now she wondered if she wasn't meant to live anywhere but Bogotá.

"I'm seeing our capital for the first time because of you," Aguja said.

"So what do you think?"

"With this traffic and pollution I have a better idea why you want to leave."

"That was never what bothered me about this place."

They returned to the apartment building after dusk, a light in the living room window bright as fire. She rang the bell again, and this time her father's voice came quick over the intercom. *Papá* was all she needed to say. In seconds the door opened and he was pulling his daughter to his chest, separating only so he could touch her face, hold her shoulders, study her eyes and know she was safe, unchanged, the child he knew. In trying to hug him with the force of her life, she realized how weak she was, exhausted, hungry. She turned from her father to introduce Aguja. Her father looked concerned but took her cue, shook Aguja's hand, thanked him for helping Talia, and invited him inside. Aguja responded that he knew Talia's and Mauro's time together was limited. He didn't want to intrude. He needed to get back to Barichara anyway.

Talia had already paid him what she promised but was grateful her father pulled out his wallet and handed over all the bills inside so Aguja could buy gas and food for the journey. She left Mauro to walk Aguja to his motorcycle. He slid onto the seat. She resisted the impulse to climb on too. Touching the string around her neck, she thanked him for bringing her home.

"If you ever find yourself back in Barichara, ask for me." He offered his hand to shake, but she stepped in to kiss his cheek, rough, unshaven, sticky with sweat. She wouldn't forget his smell. "You'll be okay, niña. It's like driving these mountain roads. You can't see what's ahead if you keep looking in the rearview mirror."

There was a new feeling. A coming to the end of something while knowing it was the beginning of something else. Her last night at home with her father. The only home that had been truly theirs, not her grandmother's house, which had been left to her mother. This was the apartment Mauro rented with two small bedrooms, a sitting area and kitchen with space for a small table. They'd lived there almost a year, but it still felt like a wrong fit, something they outgrew even before they arrived, a place of no memories, at least until tonight, and suddenly it felt like the only home she'd ever need.

He cooked one of his simple meals for her. The warmth of the stove reached every corner of the apartment. She showered away days of filth, sat on her bed in fresh clothes, the suitcase her father prepared resting beside the door. She thought of places she'd slept in order to arrive at this night, remembering the prison school, the nuns her father said called many times asking if she'd found her way back to him. Her homecoming was a secret they'd both have to keep. He didn't ask for details of her escape. He wouldn't know the things she'd done, the lies she'd told, what she'd stolen. Memories she hoped to drop from the sky the minute her plane left their mountains and crossed the ocean.

As they ate, she watched her father, this man who was both young and old. He'd lost weight in her absence. His skin darkened in its hollows. After she left, he would continue to transform even more with age and time. She wanted to memorize him as he was now.

Her father would not let them be downhearted on this, their final night before she was due to leave. He played music and lifted her from the sofa to dance with him the way he taught her when he first came to live at Perla's house, carrying her small feet on his toes until her body discovered its instinct for rhythm.

She was so tired, but she didn't want to sleep, wishing they could still go up to the roof of Perla's house for a farewell to the city lights. In the new apartment of no sunrises or sunsets, all they had was their small windows with a view to the street.

When she woke, it was still dark. She went to her father's room, saw him sleeping atop his blanket, hands folded over his heart like a man at his own funeral. She wanted to wake him so he could tell her one more time about Chía, the guardian of night. She wanted to ask if the goddess would still watch over her when she was so far away from their land, but instead she let her father sleep.

TWENTY-EIGHT

They were just another parent and child in an airport terminal full of goodbyes. They entered as conspirators, calm, trying not to show their fear that she could be arrested. Police patrolled. Working dogs sniffed baggage. She knew from TV programs there were hidden cameras all around. They approached the counter. When it was her turn, she slid over her blue passport. At fifteen she was old enough not to have to travel as an unaccompanied minor. The airline attendant looked over the top of her glasses at Mauro and asked their relation.

"I'm her father." He handed over his ID so the woman could compare their last names.

"Who will meet you at the airport when you arrive?" she asked Talia.

"My mother."

In her handbag, an envelope of cash her father withdrew from the bank. Her heart quivered as the airline employee studied her passport picture, then scanned the bar code. Talia had seen enough movies to write her own scene of a police stampede surrounding and removing her in handcuffs. But nothing like that happened. The woman returned Talia's passport with a boarding pass tucked inside and wished her a good trip.

Relief, but only temporarily, because she still had to get through customs and security. Her first time flying since her arrival as a baby. She felt dispirited. The composure she'd practiced in the taxi all the way to the airport, clutching her father's hand on the vinyl upholstery between them, was gone. Mauro must have sensed this because he led her to a column along the corridor, held her close, and whispered that she was safe, nobody would take her away. She would get on that plane, and in a few hours she would be in her mother's arms.

"What if I want to come back?"

"You can. You have two places to call home."

A goodbye is always too brief, or maybe she'd been saying goodbye since she came to Colombia, aware for as long as she'd collected memories that her place there was only provisional.

"What if I don't love my mother the way I love you?"

"You will. You do. When you see her you will remember."

"And my brother and sister?"

"They are a part of you too."

"I don't want to go." This came from some unknowable place but now felt truer than anything. "Don't make me leave you."

Her father was quiet. He knew that if she stayed the authorities would come for her and send her back to the school on the mountain or another one like it. And even after she completed her sentence, restlessness would never leave her until she returned to her point of origin. She could not leave, but she could not stay.

His eyes were dry, but she knew it was because he'd learned to cry without tears. They said all the things a father and daughter say to each other when they are not sure when or how they will ever see each other again.

How many years would pass between this moment and that one?

How would they be changed by a life apart?

She already felt aged by the day. No longer fifteen but as if she'd lived a decade more and understood, though she didn't yet know how, that this would be the morning she would dream of, guard in her palms like a loose pearl during her future loneliness.

How stupid she was to think leaving would be as easy as handing over her ticket and finding her seat on the plane. She did not yet know she would mourn this morning like a death.

Mauro watched her as far as the airport perimeters would allow. When she reached the front of the line and gave her passport to the customs agent, she turned and saw him peering from the corner along the last visible stretch of airport tunnel. She had to go on without him. He would stay at the airport until her plane was in the clouds, he'd said. Her phone was programmed to dial him with a single touch should she be detained. They'd prepared in every way for the worst possible outcome, but everything was happening faster than expected. The agent waved her on. At the security checkpoint, while others were asked to step aside to have their bags individually examined, she passed through with ease. Her father was out of sight, but she knew he was still close.

From her window seat the city unspooled, dissolving like salt in water. The exquisite madness of the cordilleras, bottle-green valleys devoured by doughy clouds until there was nothing to see but white and more white. When the pilot announced they'd left Colombian airspace, a man a few rows back started singing the national anthem but only made it through the first verse about goodness coming from pain, not to the parts about battles and bloodshed. Over the blue ribbons of the Caribbean she managed to sleep. When she woke, the plane was shaking in descent over another gray city. No mountains. Only flatness winged by obsidian rivers scabbed in concrete and steel.

. . .

The night before, she'd told her father she was afraid she and her family wouldn't recognize one another at the airport.

"You will know them when you see them, and they will know you."

She drifted through immigration and out of the baggage claim area, past another agent who took the paper form from her hand without any questions and through to a hall packed with excited faces, many holding signs, balloons, flower bouquets.

"How will they know me?" she'd asked her father, when they'd only ever seen her face crammed into the inches of a photograph or screen.

How will they know me?

In the end that was also a beginning, there was recognition beyond features and gestures. A love born before any of the siblings, that delivered her from her father back to her mother.

The mother held her child, both wanting to express everything with their embrace. Her mother's arms were sinewy around her ribcage. She was shorter than Talia had believed. Her scent— powder, violets, something else—familiar yet new. Her earrings pressed hard against her daughter's cheek, as she hummed, *mi hija, mi hija*, like a song.

Her brother and sister cloaked them with their bodies.

Her mother's employers sent them to receive Talia in a big chauffeured car that waited for them outside the airport. Her sister and brother muttered to each other in English in the back seat. Her mother sat at her side, held her hand, reached for her face to kiss her cheek. Talia stiffened, remembering she was in a car full of strangers who were also her family. They told her that the next day there would be a party for her at the home of some friends in the town where they'd lived for many years. Everyone was excited to meet her.

She took in New Jersey, level and highwayed. So many lanes and cars, square buildings and a hazy horizon. Far from Colombia with its equatorial pulse and steepled mountains. She tried to restrain her tears, but they fell fast.

Her mother stroked her hair. "It's too much," she said. "I'm sorry. I should have known. We will take it slow. Tranquila, mi amor. No llores."

Their home was a small house behind a larger one. A swimming pool sat in between. A boy watched from a window as the car pulled into the driveway. They showed her the bedroom she'd share with her sister, painted alabaster, windows overlooking rosebushes, no brick panorama like the one she left that morning. How would she sleep there, one night, a dozen nights, the hundreds or thousands of nights that would spread before her in an endless calendar of days waiting for something, she didn't know what. Another departure? Another arrival? She was no longer sure where her journey began or where it should end.

TWENTY-NINE

Mauro waited in the airport for almost twelve hours, long after Talia's plane left their soil and landed in that foreign space. She called when she arrived at her new house, her voice laden with uncertainty though she kept saying, "It's beautiful here, Papá. So beautiful." She thought her father was back at their apartment, but he was still by the checkpoint where he'd left her, watching other families in their last seconds together before parting. For the first hours after her takeoff, despite the solace of knowing that she hadn't been detained, he worried there would be some malfunction or even a bomb threat; a reason for her plane to have to loop around in the sky and return home. Even after the airline employees told him her flight had landed safely in the United States he waited on a plastic bench with a shameful wish that she'd decided, instead of going home with her family, to take the next flight back to him.

They were thoughts that came with the heartsickness of separation. He knew such fantasies well, from their earliest incarnations when he was sent to the campo by his mother to when he found himself in the detention center and when the Americans dispatched him back to his country alone. His daughter had left him, but she still came to him in his sleep, asking him to tell her stories about the lake, about Chiminigagua, about the ancestors, begging him to bring them with him when he arrived to meet her in the north.

At first, her calls were frequent. Daily. Sometimes twice, in the morning and before she went to sleep. She reported everything about her new life, gossiping affectionately about her mother and her siblings. She suspected her mother was a little frightened of her. Not because she might be dangerous, but as if she were some breakable object, like a centuries-old museum artifact on loan between nations.

Her brother and sister, she said, took her on outings to Manhattan, where she felt choked by crowds and buildings taller than their highest mountains, where the subway vibrations reminded her of the tremors she felt underfoot back home, Chibchacum adjusting his load; and to the beach, wide as a field and full of people, sand coarse and mottled with cigarette butts, the Atlantic water inky and cold.

Her English improved beyond television and movie dialogue. Her sister became her teacher, instructing her to read pages of novels aloud for an hour each night. On weekends, her family took her to the other town where their good friends lived and the adults, too, treated her as if she were a special thing, precious and symbolic as an emerald ensconced in gold. She worried they hadn't yet figured out that she was ordinary, she told her father, exceptional only in her ability to do harm and to run away, and was terrified that someone would learn of her crime and time at the prison school and tell her mother.

The funny thing, she said, was that back home she felt she had so much to say, but in her new country everyone kept commenting how quiet she was. She even heard her mother describe her as shy. She worried she'd left her real self with her father and the girl who flew to the United States in her place, though she wore the same face, was someone else.

• • •

A few weeks after her departure, Mauro received a call from the police. They learned Talia had left the country. They knew the day and the hour, and he prayed they hadn't searched security camera footage showing them together at the airport as he prepared to send her off. He was able to fake shock, which the police seemed to believe, since Elena had been the one to purchase the plane ticket. They asked if he'd heard from her. He said he hadn't. They asked if he knew how to reach Elena, and he lied that they hadn't spoken in years. And so the call turned to one of sympathy.

"I am sorry to have to give you this bad news," the officer said. "Now that your daughter has fled the country to be with her mother, you may never see either of them again."

Elena called to thank Mauro for the Virgin statue he'd sent, for the photographs and for the letter he'd tucked into the envelope with them. He waited for her to say more, but she was quiet. Then she thanked him for the years he'd cared for Talia. Said every day was a revelation of who she was as a young woman. Despite the distance and years apart, she'd somehow convinced herself she knew their daughter well. Now she understood that child was fiction. The daughter Elena was getting to know was smarter, wiser, as lovely and self-governing as a wildflower.

Without Talia between them now, Mauro worried the threads that bound him and Elena would fray to nothing. He felt a dam of urgency break in him.

"I'll find a way back." He didn't know if she understood or if she would even believe him. He only hoped that when he made it to the other side, she would be waiting.

•   •   •

The apartment was packed and ready for its next occupancy. The boxes with the few things that mattered to them held in a storage unit where he'd paid the year in advance. After Talia left, Mauro did months of research. Enough time had passed since his deportation that he could apply for legal reentry. He submitted the paperwork and was approved for an appointment at the US embassy, which gave him hope that his past offenses might be pardoned. He took the day off and wore his best clothes, brought a file of photos of his family and copies of Nando's and Talia's birth certificates. He told the consular officer he had two US-born children and his deportation had caused substantial hardship on their mother. He'd read about another deported father in Nicaragua with a similar family situation who was granted a special waiver with the help of some advocacy group. But Mauro still had no sponsor waiting for him on the other side and now had nothing in Colombia proving any incentive to return. His request was refused. He could reapply, the officer said, or wait until his American children were old enough to petition for a parent visa, but the arrests on Mauro's record made it unlikely he'd ever be granted entry again.

He considered other potential routes. First to the United States by way of Canada, but ruled it out when he learned the two countries share immigration information. A flight to Jamaica or the Bahamas since neither required visas of Colombians. Or by boat to Panama through the Darién Gap and San Blas Islands, by bus and train the rest of the way north. The more he stared at those borders on maps, the more absurd it seemed that outsiders succeeded in declaring possession of these lands with national lines, as if Creation could ever be divided and owned.

The best and most reliable route, he concluded, was through Mexico. He knew a man from his meetings, which he attended every night since Talia's departure, who'd made the trip through the Chihuahuan desert successfully only to return to Colombia because he missed the wife and child he left behind too much. The journey was hard on the body, he warned Mauro. *If you go that way, rest for many days before crossing. When you're ready, dress like a gentleman on his way to church and pray one thousand rosaries. When you finish, you will be on the other side.*

For months, he cut meals to save pesos. Sold his ruanas and trinkets leftover from Perla's house to tourists at the flea market and took extra shifts at his job whenever he could. He turned the apartment back over to the landlord. Bought two plane tickets. One to Panama and from there, another to Mexico. The man who'd taken the desert route told him that from the capital he needed to head to the frontera and wait in a town named, of all things, Colombia. A man he knew there would help Mauro cross over. Entering the United States again without inspection or admission, as they say, could get him barred from the country forever.

It was worth wagering, Mauro decided, even if just to see his family one more time.

A dewy morning back in the same airport where he'd held his daughter before she left for her new life. He waited to board his own flight alone, this time as a free man and not as the prisoner he was when last returned to his country. Talia did not yet know that he was coming. He hadn't wanted to share his plans, fearing his trip would be interrupted and he'd be forced back to Bogotá to begin the journey all over again.

He was not viewed as a criminal in any country but the one where his family lived. He would be safe until he arrived at the national line, and then he'd see how far his luck would travel. Until then, he guarded a new picture in his mind: Nochebuena. Their first as a complete family. Parents preparing a meal together for their three children, singing songs they used to sing, dancing the way they used to dance. Falling asleep with love in their hearts. The next morning, one of thousands with which they'd mend the years torn from their family pages, creating new stories in place of elisions. No more anguish of time lost. Nothing would matter but each new day and the ones to come.

THIRTY

I started writing the chronicle of our lives because it's important to leave a record. For us, if for nobody else, because everyone has a secret self truer than the parts you see.

One day in early September, just before she was to start at her new high school, I saw my sister sitting with our mother in the garden near the creek knoll. I could tell by the way they faced each other, the way our mother's gaze never moved while Talia's searched around, often fixing on the blades of grass she held between her fingers, that she was confessing what she'd already shared with me, the crime she committed back home, how they'd sent her to a prison for girls on the edge of irredeemable, how she'd wanted to hide this secret forever because she thought we couldn't love her in spite of it, even when I told her I understood; we all have breaking points, we all have regrets and maybe more instances we don't regret that society tells us we should. I told her I understood what it was to want to create justice to fix an injustice even if my justice could be considered a crime. I know what it is to hurt and to feel hurt on behalf of others. I tried to say this in my best Spanish and asked if she understood, if she believed me, and she said she did.

I didn't let myself watch their entire exchange. I went to our living room, where my brother was sketching faces, and watched him until our mother and sister returned to the cottage.

I want to say that our family entered a new era, not just of reunification, but of truth-telling that began with our mother, who told me a few days before our sister's arrival what happened to her years before when she worked at a restaurant, at the hands of the man who hired and paid her. Maybe I sensed something like this had happened to her because I didn't react with tears. I only listened, and when she was through, her face slack as a sheet hanging in the rain, I held her and told her I was sorry for being too small to protect her, but she said it was the very reason she was telling me now, to protect me from something similar happening, and most of all, to defend me from silence. In time, she would tell my brother and sister, she said, and our father too.

That night I thought about how love comes paired with failures, apologies for deficiencies. The only remedy is compassion. I thought about this again when my sister told me of her crime and how she'd run away from her school on the mountain in order to catch her flight to this country, because she thought if we knew or if she asked to postpone the flight we'd change our minds about wanting her to live with us; how she hitched rides across the departments of Santander, Boyacá, and Cundinamarca, and slept beside strangers until she made her way back to our father, and before she left that final morning for the airport, she wrote a letter to Horacio, the man she burned, saying she was very sorry she hurt him and wished him a good life though she did not expect to be forgiven, and she asked our father to mail it for her, though the mail in Colombia was notoriously unreliable and there was no way to know if the envelope, which she'd addressed to the restaurant where he once worked, made it to his hands.

• • •

By this time, we knew our father was on his way to us. He made it to Laredo, a border city we'd heard about on the news due to all the deportations of people who arrived seeking asylum from danger in their homelands, the separated families, parents and children torn from one another and placed in detention. But he was safe, only hours from where he began his first journey in this country with our mother and me. He called to say he'd made it to a migrant shelter run by some nuns where they let him rest. Someone there connected him with a volunteer group that told him buses and trains were too risky. Through their network they arranged a series of car rides and safe houses so he could cross the country. Till then, we waited. Our mother didn't sleep much those nights, and sometimes I left the room I shared with my sister to sit with her on her bed and listen as she told me it was a scary thing to have all your prayers answered.

They delivered him to our mother's employers' gate. I saw him walking up the driveway. My brother and sister were at school, and our mother was in the main house. I went to him, but my last steps shrinking our gap were slow and heavy. He said my name. I could see he was nervous that I would reject him. I went to him and reached around his body for a hug. I am almost as tall as he is now, but I was small again and his scent came back to me; we were no longer in the driveway but in some apartment I hadn't thought about in years yet no time had passed at all.

I led him to the main house and saw his eyes take in the proportions of everything, the softness and beigeness of the walls and upholstery, every rug and painting and decorative detail as he trailed me from room to room in the otherwise empty house and I called for my mother. Then she was in front of us, a laundry basket in her hands. She dropped it when she saw him, her face rumpling with a dry cry as he ran to her and held her and she made kitten-ish whimpers in the fabric of his shirt. In my waking memory, I'd never seen them like this, had no recollection of them touching or even speaking face-to-face, but an intimate familiarity came over us; I felt a river current, a serpentine wind, an artery of lightning pass through my parents and through me. I didn't know how long they'd be like this, but it didn't matter; I already felt the moment become eternal.

For now we still live in the cottage until we can save for a big-ger place. You may have noticed I haven't told you the name of the town. That's because as long as we're here, we're vulnerable. Until something changes in the laws and the climate so that people under-stand we are not the enemy. Our family is whole now, but there is no day that passes without anxiousness that I may come home to find my mother or father have been taken into custody. Or that the one taken could be me.

Our father is doing handiwork and repairs for a friend of our mother's bosses. When he's not at his new job, just as my mother and sister have done, and my brother with the pages he handed over, our father has begun to tell me the story of him, of how our family came to be, which I've tried to write here, though the stories keep coming, so I know the book of our lives will continue to grow with truth and time.

It's not that the sum of these pages can tell everything about us. There are things we will never share with one another, that will re-main unnamed or unspoken. Things I save for private journals, like how I wonder if I will ever find the kind of love I want, a love that at least at its inception resembles what our parents felt when they discovered each other and trusted each other enough to travel to a new world together. There are innumerable joys left out of these pages. Sorrows too. A life rendered will always be incomplete.

Soon after our father arrived we went to a party in our old neighborhood and introduced him to our friends from the basement days. When a cumbia came on, he asked our mother to dance, and we watched our parents sway, finding each other's rhythm as if they'd never fallen out of step, as if the past fifteen years were only a dance interrupted waiting for the next song to play. I wondered about the matrix of separation and dislocation, our years bound to the phantom pain of a lost homeland, because now that we are together again that particular hurt and sensation that something is missing has faded. And maybe there is no nation or citizenry; they're just territories mapped in place of family, in place of love, the infinite country.

ACKNOWLEDGMENTS

To the families who see aspects of their experiences reflected in these pages: You are my heroes. I wrote this book for you.

To victims and survivors of every kind of violence, and to the displaced and the disappeared: I carry you in my heart.

My thanks to Ayesha Pande, agent extraordinaire, and the Pande Literary team; to the always visionary Lauren Wein; Amy Guay, Meredith Vilarello, Alexandra Primiani, Morgan Hoit, Jessica Chin, Alison Forner, and everyone at Avid Reader Press and Simon & Schuster for your work on this book and for such a warm welcome.

My thanks to the John Simon Guggenheim Memorial Foundation for their generous support of my research and writing of this novel; to Viet Thanh Nguyen and *Ploughshares* for publishing an early excerpt; to my colleagues and students at the University of Miami, especially M. Evelina Galang and Chantel Acevedo; and to the dear friends who've encouraged me along the way.

My gratitude to my family in the United States and Colombia; to my nieces, the youngest Engel writers; to my husband, John Henry, for so much love and laughter; to S, G, and M, my adored companions.

Above all, I thank my mother and father for their love, their stories, and for holding on to each other no matter what.

ABOUT THE AUTHOR

PATRICIA ENGEL is the author of *The Veins of the Ocean*, winner of the Dayton Literary Peace Prize; *It's Not Love, It's Just Paris*, winner of an International Latino Book Award; and *Vida*, a finalist for the PEN/Hemingway and Young Lions Fiction Awards, a *New York Times* Notable Book, and winner of the Premio Biblioteca de Narrativa Colombiana. She is a recipient of fellowships from the Guggenheim Foundation and the National Endowment for the Arts. Her stories appear in *The Best American Short Stories*, *The Best American Mystery Stories*, *The O. Henry Prize Stories*, and elsewhere. Born to Colombian parents, Patricia teaches at the University of Miami.